CW01630646

Rafael Sabatini, c [illegible] ed heroes, was born in Ital [illegible] tugal and Switzerland. He [illegible] by which time he was fluent [illegible] to write in English, claiming that 'all the best stories are written in English'.

His writing career was launched in the 1890s with a collection of short stories, and it was not until 1902 that his first novel was published. His fame, however, came with Scaramouche, the much-loved story of the French Revolution, which became an international bestseller. Captain Blood followed soon after, which resulted in a renewed enthusiasm for his earlier work.

For many years a prolific writer, he was forced to abandon writing in the 1940s through illness and he eventually died in 1950.

Sabatini is best-remembered for his heroic characters and high-spirited novels, many of which have been adapted into classic films, including Scaramouche, Captain Blood and The Sea Hawk starring Errol Flynn.

He was also an expert on Renaissance Italy and wrote the definitve biography of Cesare Borgia, along with other notable non-fiction texts including Torquemada and The Spanish Inquisition.

TITLES BY THE SAME AUTHOR
ALL PUBLISHED BY HOUSE OF STRATUS

Fiction:

Anthony Wilding
The Banner of the Bull
Bardelys the Magnificent
Bellarion
The Black Swan
Captain Blood
The Carolinian
Chivalry
The Chronicles of Captain Blood
Columbus
Fortune's Fool
The Gamester
The Gates of Doom
The Hounds of God
The Justice of the Duke
The Lion's Skin
The Lost King
Love-at-Arms
The Marquis of Carabas
The Minion
The Nuptials of Corbal
The Romantic Prince
Scaramouche
Scaramouche the King-maker
The Sea Hawk
The Shame of Motley
The Snare
St Martin's Summer
The Stalking-horse
The Strolling Saint
The Sword of Islam
The Tavern Knight
The Trampling of the Lilies
Turbulent Tales
Venetian Masque

Non-fiction:

Heroic Lives
The Historical Nights' Entertainment
King in Prussia
The Life of Cesare Borgia
Torquemada and the Spanish Inquisition

The Nuptials of Corbal

Rafael Sabatini

HOUSE OF STRATUS

Copyright © Rafael Sabatini 1927
© 2012 House of Stratus

All rights reserved. No part of this publication may be reproduced, stored in a retrieval system, or transmitted, in any form, or by any means (electronic, mechanical, photocopying, recording, or otherwise), without the prior permission of the publisher. Any person who does any unauthorised act in relation to this publication may be liable to criminal prosecution and civil claims for damages.

The right of Rafael Sabatini to be identified as the author of this work has been asserted.

This edition published in 2012 by House of Stratus, an imprint of
Stratus Books Ltd., Lisandra House, Fore Street,
Looe, Cornwall, PL13 1AD, U.K.
www.houseofstratus.com

Typeset by House of Stratus.

A catalogue record for this book is available from the British Library and the Library of Congress.

ISBN 07551-1548-1
EAN 978-07551-1548-8

This book is sold subject to the condition that it shall not be lent, resold, hired out, or otherwise circulated without the publisher's express prior consent in any form of binding, or cover, other than the original as herein published and without a similar condition being imposed on any subsequent purchaser, or bona fide possessor.

This is a fictional work and all characters are drawn from the author's imagination. Any resemblance or similarities to persons either living or dead are entirely coincidental.

Chapter One

Shadows moved behind the broad lattice that formed the upper part of the heavy wooden doors at the gallery's end. Those nearest, observing this and knowing what it portended, caught their breath. From these apprehension ran like a wave over the groups assembled in that long narrow avenue of doom, stilling their chatter, as it went, until in a moment all was silence.

Upon that silence the rasping of a key in its lock rang like a pistol shot. One of the ponderous wings of the great door swung inwards. The turnkey entered, brawny and swarthy, his blue shirt gaping away from a broad hairy chest, a fur bonnet on his cropped head, a yellow bloodhound at his heels. He stood aside on the broad platform at the head of the steps, to give passage to a brisk young gentleman in a tight black frock and a round black hat that was adorned by a buckle in front and a cockade at the side. A paper in his hand drew the eyes – some scared, some apathetic, some proudly indifferent and some defiantly scornful – of the hundred or so men and women assembled there from their various quarters for the daily purpose of hearing that paper's contents. For this slim young gentleman, Robert Wolf, clerk of the Revolutionary Tribunal, was the adjutant of the Public Accuser. His paper bore the list over whose preparation Fouquier-Tinville had laboured half the night, in his little room in the Tower of Caesar: that room of the Palais de Justice where he had his being, where he worked and slept, which he never quitted save to dine and to discharge before the Tribunal the dread functions of his office. For a man of unremitting zeal was this Fouquier-Tinville, a conscientious public servant who spared himself so little in his labours on behalf of the Nation, that in the pursuit of duty he neglected himself, his health, his wife and his children.

The Citizen Wolf stepped briskly to the edge of the platform, placed himself so that the light should fall upon his paper, and disposed himself to read the names of those whom Fouquier-Tinville summoned that morning to judgment: the *fournée,* or bakers batch, as it was called in the cynical jargon of the day.

Having chosen his position, the clerk waited until three men who followed him should come to a standstill, so that the hollow ring of their steps upon the planking should not obscure his utterance. Not on that account did they hurry themselves. Two of them, men of middle age, both dressed in black, one tall and portly, the other short and wizened, took their time deferentially from the third who, walking a little in advance, appeared to conduct them.

This was Chauvinière, the Nivernais deputy, a tall slim fellow, of an age not over thirty, of a certain vigorous elegance of figure and poise, of a certain elegance even in his dress. He wore a riding-coat with broad lapels and silver buttons, the tails of which reached almost to the heels of his Hessian boots. Spotless buckskins cased his long, lean legs so closely that every muscle was defined, and a cravat of spotless white clothed his neck stiffly to the chin. He was girt by a tricolour sash, and a tricolour cockade adorned his grey hat, which was cocked in front, *à la* Henri IV, and surmounted by a panache of black plumes. Thus were his office and his sansculottism advertised, and if some there were who thought them advertised too elegantly for sincerity, our gentleman was not to be perturbed. His sansculottism stood too high, had been too fully proven to be shaken by any gibes at his apparel, whilst his arrogance, audacity and self-assurance were a panoply against vulgar criticism. These qualities were to be read in his lean, sallow countenance with its high-bridged nose, its curled upper lip and its keen light eyes under level black brows. There was a certain rallishness in his air, an indescribable quality that proclaimed him half-gentleman, half-valet, half-wolf, half-fox.

With a leisureliness that took no account either of the waiting clerk or of the agonised suspense and the pounding of a hundred hearts in that assembly, which he eyed so coldly, Chauvinière selected his point of vantage, at a little distance from Robert Wolf, and descended the first step, so that his two companions in black immediately behind him, obtained, from the summit of the platform, a clear view over his head.

His keen eyes raked the gallery and the men and women in that throng, most of whom were so scrupulously dressed that, saving for the absence of powder from their heads, they might have been gathered together for a *lévee*. This was a daily miracle performed upon slender enough resources by the prisoners in the Conciergerie.

The deputy's hungry eyes quested on until they came at last to rest upon Mademoiselle de Montsorbier, standing slim and straight beside the chair into which her mother had nervelessly collapsed. Incredibly fearless and resolute she stood, with scarcely loss of colour to her lovely face. But the blue-green eyes dilated a little and flickered as they met the deputy's kindling glance. Her slight bosom moved perceptibly under its crossed muslin fichu, to betray a sudden agitation which not even the advent of the list had been able to arouse.

Chauvinière half-turned to the men in black behind him. He said something in a low voice into an obsequiously lowered ear, and with his silver-mounted cane – the only weapon he carried – he deliberately pointed. Three pairs of eyes followed the direction of the pointing, and Mademoiselle de Montsorbier stiffened under that volley of glances to whose purport she possessed no clue, but which instinctively she felt to bode no good.

Then the pointing cane was lowered, and the three men ranged themselves decorously, as Robert Wolf began to call the names of the doomed. His voice droned emotionlessly. Like Fouquier-Tinville himself, he was simply a part of the great revolutionary machine. There was no personal responsibility in what he did, and it was not for him to indulge feelings and emotions over actions that were not his own. He was a voice, no more: the summoning voice of the Tribunal. Because practised in his functions, he paused after each name, so as to allow the hush to be resumed, lest the next name should be lost to his audience in the sounds that ensued upon each of his utterances. To answer each summons there would be now a gasp, now a rustling stir about a person named, now a sob of terror, sometimes a laugh, occasionally a reckless answer, and more occasionally still an outcry of hysterical panic quickly sinking into shuddering sobs.

The voice droned on: "The *ci-devant* Marquis de La Tourette."

The Marquis, a middle-aged exquisite in a blue coat with silver lace, threw up his head – the handsome head that so soon would leave his shoulders – and sharply caught his breath. In an instant he recovered. He remembered what was due to his blood and his self-respect. He shrugged and smiled in deprecation, for all that his face was of the colour of chalk.

"It will break the monotony," he said softly to a neighbour, as the next name was being called.

"The *ci-devant* Comtesse de Montsorbier." Madame de Montsorbier, a slender little woman of fifty, half-rose from her chair, beginning an inarticulate cry on which she seemed to choke. Then her knees were loosened, and she sank down again, leaning sideways against her daughter. Mademoiselle de Montsorbier, rigid now and piteously white, set protecting arms about her half-swooning mother, listening the while to the clerk's voice and waiting to hear her own name, almost hoping to hear it, in her selfless anxiety to accompany her mother before the Tribunal and thence to the scaffold. All that she realised was that in her agony, the frail woman who had borne her would require her as she had never required her yet. Solicitude for her mother effaced all consideration of herself and her own fate. That was the mettle of Mademoiselle de Montsorbier, and her deepest dismay was not reached until the list had come to an end without her own name having been pronounced.

The summoned twenty were passing out, some faltering, some in grim resolve, a few with histrionically jaunty ease after brief farewells.

Mademoiselle de Montsorbier heard as in a dream the Marquis de La Tourette's pleasant level voice, addressing the Duc de Chaulnes.

"For once I take precedence of you, Monseigneur."

To which his Grace retorted lightly: "To my infinite regret, since we lose your pleasant company, dear Marquis. But we shall rejoin you presently, I trust in Paradise. My compliments to Fouquier-Tinville."

Two gendarmes, coming she knew not whence, surged suddenly before her.

"The *ci-devant* Montsorbier," said one of them, and set a hand upon the drooping shoulder of madame.

Mademoiselle de Montsorbier turned to him, deserted for once by her self-possession, and unable in her mental distress to marshal her tumultuous thoughts into coherent expression.

"But it is my mother! There is some error. She cannot go without me. You see how feeble she is. My name has not been called. It is an omission. You see that it is an omission. You will tell them that it is an omission. You will let me go with her."

Thus, in a confused torrent, the phrases tumbled from her lips.

The man looked at her sullenly, dubiously, his nether lip projected. He lowered his head. "Not our affair." He shook the Countess who was not more than half-conscious. "You are to come along, *citoyenne.*"

"But I may go with her? I may go with her?"

"It is not in the order."

Mademoiselle de Montsorbier wrung her hands. "But you can explain to your Tribunal!"

"Ah, bah! What's your hurry to sneeze into the basket? Your turn will come soon enough, *citoyenne.* Lend a hand, Gaston."

Between them the two men dragged the Countess to her feet, and half-carried, half-led her away. The girl sprang after them.

"I may come, too; may I not? I may—"

A blow in the stomach from the elbow of one of the guards cut short her breath, and sent her hurtling backwards. "Faith! You're too cursedly persistent! You make yourself a nuisance, my girl!"

She reeled to the wooden chair the Countess had vacated, struck her legs against its edge, and fell into it rather than sat down.

"Mother!" she gasped aloud, when at last her breath returned. "Mother!"

White-faced she sat, in stony, tearless grief, her long fine hands clutched between her knees.

Just so, a month ago, had her father been rent from them, to take his trial; and hers it had been since then to comfort and sustain her mother. Now her mother, too, was gone, and alone; that frail lady, who had never been alone, who was in all things helpless. She would not return. None of those who were summoned ever did return; and they were few, very few, who escaped the chill caress of the guillotine to be set at liberty.

Why had she been left? Why had it been denied her to continue to the end the only useful purpose she could serve in life? What now remained for her?

A voice was speaking at her elbow, a crisp, level voice, not unpleasant although pitched in a tone almost ironical.

"This is the young woman who claims your attention, citizens. You observe her listlessness, her unnatural pallor, the vacancy of her stare. Perform your office. It is not for me to direct you, or even to suggest; but for you to judge."

She swung half-round, looking up, challenge, defiance, alarm all blending in her glance, like some trapped wild creature suddenly confronted by its trapper. She met the light eyes of Chauvinière, piercing, mocking eyes which she had grown to hate, and even to fear, she who had never before feared anything in all her proud young life.

A half-dozen times in the last three weeks had she found these eyes upon her in a questing, measuring, soullessly appraising glance, which had scorched her from head to foot. Twice already had he found occasion to speak to her as he passed through the prisoners' gallery on a visit which appeared to have no other object but that of addressing her. Each time she had commanded herself so as to dissemble from him her resentment at the insult which his look and word conveyed, and so as to answer him with an icy dignity which placed a whole world between them. She would command herself now. He should never guess her fear of him, this dishonouring fear for which she loathed herself.

The two men in black were gravely considering her, the taller one leaning forward a little. He extended a plump hand, and took her wrist.

"Your pulse, *citoyenne.*"

"My pulse?" She heard herself ask the question in a distant voice, and knew by the drumming of her temples that her pulses were galloping. Then, above considerations of herself, rose again the momentarily whelmed memory of her bereavement. "You, monsieur ... citizen, citizen-deputy! They have taken madame my mother, and by an omission I have been left. Give order, monsieur, I implore you, that my name be added to the list of the day—"

"Ah!" said Chauvinière, with so singular an emphasis that it arrested her intercession.

He looked at the men in black with a significant lift of his brows. "You hear her, citizen-doctors! Is that the request of a young woman who is sane? To desire – indeed, to implore – death at that age, when life unfolds itself like a perfumed rose, when the blood runs warm and clear! Is not that a sufficient confirmation of what already I suspected? But"—and again there was that flash of mockery from those light eyes—"it is not for me to influence your opinion. You must form judgment for yourselves. Proceed! Proceed!" He waved a hand, a hand that was long and slender as an aristocrat's, and as graceful in its gesture, which subtly blended invitation with command.

The doctors sighed and grunted.

"For my own part," said the shorter one, "I do not like her eyes. This wild, hunted look, and this general expression of distraction ... hem! Hem!"

"And then her pallor, as the citizen-deputy says," put in the other. "Most unnatural! And this pulse! But feel it for yourself."

She laughed. It was the laugh of a bitterness too sharp for tears.

"Unnatural! My pallor, my pulse, my hunted look! Unnatural! And my mother has just been taken from me, to judgment and the scaffold. You would have me calm, messieurs? Gay, perhaps? My mother—"

"Sh, my child!" The little doctor's hand was on her brow, his thumb was doing something with her eyelids. But his manner was soothing, almost hypnotic. "Do not exalt yourself, *citoyenne.* Calm, if you please! Quite calm! Here is no need for transports or excitement. We are your friends, *citoyenne.* Friends." He addressed Chauvinière. "What she says, of course, is just. The excitement of the moment, the unhappy event of which she has just been the witness, her natural pain at the …" His voice trailed into silence, leaving the sentence unfinished, for Chauvinière's black brows were knit in a frown that made him shiver.

"Of course, of course," said the deputy's voice, and it was cold as ice, or – thought the little doctor despite himself – as the knife of the guillotine: cold and sharp, incisive and sinister. "It is for you to form the opinion. Not for me to direct you. But you will remember – that is, if you consider my observations worth remembering – that I brought you here precisely because I have upon other occasions witnessed these same traits in the *citoyenne*, at times when no external cause could be discerned such as may be held fortuitously to have arisen now."

The little doctor clutched at salvation. "Ah, but that is decisive," he exclaimed with complete conviction of tone. "If these symptoms – this pulse, this pallor, these twitchings, this glassy stare and … and the rest – have been manifest constantly and without adequate cause, one conclusion only is possible. At least," he added with a glance at his colleague, "that is my opinion."

"And mine," said the other sharply. "Emphatically, mine. It admits of no discussion. It leaps to the eye."

Chauvinière's lips momentarily twitched. "It is gratifying, citizen-doctors, for a layman to find his scientific suspicions confirmed by men of science. You will, then, certify the *citoyenne,* so that the Public Accuser may authorise her removal to a hospice, to the Archevêché, for instance."

"Justice demands no less," said the little man.

"And humanity," added the taller one.

"Naturally," said Chauvinière. "Justice and humanity must agree that this afflicted girl is in no case to plead, and the Revolutionary Tribunal has too high a sense of its duties to wish to arraign a person who is, be it temporarily or permanently, without the wit to defend herself. If you will send your certificate to the Public Accuser today, your responsibility in the matter ends. Citizens, there is no reason to detain you."

He inclined his head in dismissal, haughty as a prince of the old regime. The doctors bowed low and obsequiously as if to the blood royal, and turned to depart.

"Ah, but wait!" cried Mademoiselle de Montsorbier on a sudden note of sharpness. "Sirs, sirs!"

But the deputy's commanding hand waved them definitely away. Then his eyes swung slowly to the girl's face. She was on her feet now confronting him, and she was, or appeared to be, entirely fearless.

"Is it pretended that I am mad?" Her question was a challenge.

He admired her spirit, and commended the fastidiousness of the instincts which had rendered her desirable in his eyes. She was too fine, too clean-cut and delicately shaped to make appeal to a man of coarse sensibilities. His discernment had perceived in that slender lissom body a spirit over which no gross fellow could ever hope for empire. He was something of a student, this Chauvinière – who in pre-revolutionary days had been, like so many others who were on the summits now, a failure as a man of law. He was, too, something of a poet at heart, and something of an epicure in sensations. He knew that abiding beauty is of the mind, and that where beauty of the mind is absent a superficial beauty of the body will soon grow nauseous.

The spirit which she now displayed, standing tense, defiant, almost scornful to challenge him, confirmed his first discernment. He smiled a little.

"Must you quarrel with a pretence which will give you life, which will snatch you from under the knife of the guillotine? If you do, and at your age, then you are as mad as they are about to certify you."

A dozen questions leapt to her tormented mind. She uttered one.

"What is your interest in me, monsieur, that my life should be your concern?"

"Ah, that!" His dark brows went up, a faint smile illumined his face, a smile so gently wistful, that it almost rendered sweet and delicate his whole expression. "*Citoyenne,* you ask too many questions; more than it would be discreet to answer. I take my leave."

He doffed his plumed hat and bowed, then turned and walked away, erect, his head thrown back, looking neither to right nor to left upon the aristocrat prisoners who made way for him. He ignored alike the malevolent glances of the men and the insults of the women expressed in a hasty drawing aside of skirts lest they should become contaminated by contact with his person.

He was a man who succeeded by disregarding trifles.

Chapter Two

The Citizen-Deputy Chauvinière, representative in the National Convention of the constituency of Nevers, chose, as became a legislator of his notorious zeal, to make an inspection of the Archevêché, the whilom Palace of the Archbishop of Paris, now converted into a hospital for prisoners.

Baziret, the doctor in charge, conducted him, and was filled with terror by the deputy's uncompromising denunciations of the manner in which he found the place conducted, the abominable overcrowding, the mephitic atmosphere, the general insalubrity.

"This is not human," he declared, as they turned away from a suffocating gallery. "After all, they are men, not beasts; and although they have not yet been tried, already it seems they are subjected here to punishment such as the Nation could not desire for her vilest malefactors. They are flung to lie in straw like swine, men and women who are ill, some of them already dying! And you pack sixty into a space that could conveniently contain not more than thirty! It is inhuman, barbarous, almost beyond anything ever perpetrated by the despots."

Under those stern light eyes the portly Baziret trembled in body and in soul.

"What would you, citizen-deputy? Every day the authorities send me more of these sick from overcrowded prisons in which they cannot do other than fall ill. And my resources, then! They are utterly inadequate. The space at my command here is what you see. I cannot build new wings to the Archevêché."

"But you can keep clean the space you have; and you can avoid being pert with me, if you please. I dislike pertness. It is the sign of a shallow mind."

"Pert? I?" The doctor descended to further depths of panic. "Oh, but citizen-deputy, I assure you—"

"Enough!" His peremptoriness was terrific. "Also I dislike servility. It was well enough in the days of Capet. It will not serve in a glorious Age of Reason, when all men are free, when all men are equal, when all men are brothers. There are no masters now. Do you understand?"

"Oh, but perfectly, citizen-deputy."

"I congratulate you. Let us pass on." Never was demeanour of Sultan towards a slave of his household more contemptuous. "What have you above?"

"Above? Oh, above!" The doctor had fondly imagined the inspection at an end. "Oh, but nothing that deserves your trouble."

"All things deserve trouble at the hands of a zealous servant of the Nation. Make a note of that, citizen-doctor. It may stimulate your own zeal."

The browbeaten man of medicine bowed in silent awe.

The Apostle of Liberty and Fraternity continued: "Conduct me, if you please." And he waved a hand upwards. "The state of things I find here is to be the subject of a report I shall present this evening to the Convention. This scandal must be brought to an end."

The doctor, his hand upon the baluster, his foot in its neatly buckled shoe upon the first step of the staircase, paused and turned. His face was grey.

"In justice, citizen-deputy, you cannot lay this … this scandal to my charge. I—"

"You waste my time; and my time belongs to France. It is necessary to remind you of the most obvious things. You may depend, citizen-doctor, upon strictest justice. The reign of injustice ended with the abominable regime of the despots. I shall report as I find." He relented a little from his austerity. "So far I have no fault with you, personally. You have been frank. You have concealed nothing. You have placed no difficulties in the way of my investigations. All of which is in your favour. Continue so, and you shall have no cause to fear my report. What do you hide abovestairs?"

The doctor breathed freely at last. He even ventured a little laugh as he replied: "Hide? Hide, citizen-deputy? But what should I hide?"

"That is what I am asking you."

"Oh, but nothing. Nothing. All is open for your inspection." They began to ascend the broad staircase. "Here above are a few persons whom it has been necessary to segregate, a few unfortunates who have been certified as demented."

"Demented!" Chauvinière seemed surprised. "So that to a hospital in which already there is not room for the sick, they send also those who should be in a madhouse! What infamy!"

Baziret agreed as he would have agreed with anything the august deputy might say. If those upper chambers could be cleared of their tenants, he might establish there another ward, and thus relieve the congestion below. "The mad," he deplored, "take up so much room."

"I've noticed it," said Chauvinière. "They overcrowd the world."

On the upper floor the inspection was resumed. Baziret unlocked door after door of those chambers of solitary confinement, disclosing here an old man, there an elderly aristocratic woman, and in each chamber the same simple arrangement of deal chair and deal table and in a corner of the floor a mattress and blankets.

At last, to end the impatience which Chauvinière had perfectly dissembled, Baziret unlocked a door to reveal the person who was the cause of all this zeal on the deputy's part; the person for whom, or for his own ends with regard to whom, he burrowed in all that he now did and was presently to do. And so deep underground and so skilful was his burrowing that on the surface of things there was nothing to betray his labours.

Mademoiselle de Montsorbier occupied the room's only chair, which she had placed by the barred window. She turned her head as the door opened, and started a little at sight of Chauvinière, who considered her judicially, without any sign of recognition. He found her paler than her wont, her eyes a little strained, her features a trifle drawn. But in the main less changed perhaps than he had expected after the week that had passed since her mother's execution and her own removal from the Conciergerie; and the change, he observed, with that discriminating eye of his was not at all disfiguring. Suffering had heightened her spiritual, ethereal air. Inwardly he spared a sigh for the philosophic reflection that suffering is, after all, man's most refining influence.

"Who is this?" he asked coldly.

Baziret informed him, what time Chauvinière continued to regard the patient.

"Ha!" he said at last. "My faith, she does not look mad, that one."

"Alas! Often is it so with them. Their appearance deceives the shrewdest."

"But if you doctors may be deceived one way, you may also be deceived another." He fixed Baziret with eyes of terrible suspicion. "I can even imagine circumstances in which you might desire to be deceived."

Baziret shivered. "You mean, citizen?"

"Ah, bah! You understand me well enough. This girl now …"

He broke off, considering her again, chin in hand. Then abruptly, a man who takes a sudden resolve, he waved the doctor away.

"I'll talk to her," he said. "It is my duty to satisfy myself in every case where …" Again he broke off. "Wait for me at the end of the corridor. Out of earshot."

The doctor bowed again in his scared obsequiousness, and was gone. Chauvinière's eyes followed him. They were sly, mocking, contemptuous. At last he stepped within the room, and closed the door.

"That comedy is played," he said gently, as if taking her into his confidence, as if making her a partner in his intentions.

"You play comedy, monsieur?"

Calm and level came the question in that pleasantly modulated voice. It startled him. He inclined his head a little.

"To serve you, *citoyenne.*"

She had risen, and stood now straight and slim in her muslin fichu and full petticoat, which was in broad stripes of blue on grey. Her back was to the window, and the pale gold of the March sunlight, so that her face, in shadow, remained indistinct. Her voice, however, assured him of completest self-possession.

"But it is not a comedy of manners, I think."

"Of manners?" He was piqued. Her meaning escaped him, and he did not like meanings to escape him. It did not often happen. "And why not of manners, if you please?"

"Because for that you have forgotten something."

"What have I forgotten?"

"To remove your hat."

The audible arresting of his breath betrayed his amazement. Then laughter broke across his face: broadly, but silently, for he remembered the doctor at the end of the corridor.

"They are right to have certified you mad, *citoyenne,*" he said softly. "Decidedly you must leave here for a madhouse."

She shrank until her shoulders touched the bars of the window.

"What horror! What infamy! You know, you know that I am not mad. It was by your contriving that—"

"Sh! Hush! Hush! Name of a name!" His alarm was real. His eyes swept uneasily to the door. His head inclined a little, like one who listens. "Talk so, *citoyenne,* and you destroy us both."

She trilled a note or two of laughter, in mockery of him and his sudden fears.

"In this land of freedom, monsieur, in this Age of Reason of which you are one of the priests, surely a woman may destroy herself without comment if she will. And as for your destruction: can you conceive that it would concern me?"

He sighed. "I have admired your spirit, *citoyenne.* I begin to fear you have too much of it." He approached her by a step or two. "You are very young. Can you already have been so robbed of what we call illusions that you must count every man your enemy? If so, then it would be idle to protest that I am your friend; that I labour to give you back the liberty and the life which at your age should be very dear and precious; that to this end I have schemed and wrought, and to this end am ready to continue even at the risk of my own neck. If you are not convinced by the evidence already afforded you, if you are unwilling to stake upon it your life, which otherwise is forfeit, then, *citoyenne,* I had better depart again and leave you to your fate. It would imperil me too deeply to labour to persuade you: just as it might imperil me to be found bareheaded here, which is the only reason why I did not remove my hat."

Conviction of one injustice done may often temper a whole outlook. And Mademoiselle de Montsorbier feeling herself convicted now in the trivial matter of his hat, wondered whether she might not, after all, have judged him as rashly and by inferences as faulty in those other graver matters.

She considered him, and found in him now a certain dignity, which was not without appeal.

"But why," she asked quietly, "should you desire to serve me?"

A smile momentarily softened his saturnine countenance. "I do not believe a man has lived since the world began who did not at some time desire to serve one woman."

That was plain enough, and the traditions in which she had been reared rendered it an insult in her eyes. She let him see this clearly in her sudden stiffening, the up-tilting of her chin, the frown above her blue-green eyes and the angry flush that stained her delicately tinted face.

"You forget your place, sir," she told him, speaking as to an impertinent groom. "You presume insufferably."

If it stung him, he betrayed no hurt. His gentle smile grew even gentler, sadder. It was within his considerable psychological knowledge that he who would gain empire over a woman must begin by making himself her slave.

"Presume? Is it presumption to state an historical truth? Do I ask for anything? Do I demand wages for the service I proffer? I am at your command, *citoyenne,* to save your life, because ..." He paused, and made a little gesture of self-deprecation. "Because the desire to serve you, without guerdon or hope of guerdon, is stronger than myself. Is that to presume?"

"No, monsieur. It is to be incredible."

Gravely he considered her, standing there so slim and straight, a figure almost boyish save for the slight swell under her muslin fichu, her delicately featured face so supremely composed, and the sunlight behind her setting a glowing nimbus about her golden head.

"Incredible, yes," he agreed at last. "I have often been accounted that. There is a twist in my nature. My mind was cast in an ironical mould. The unexpected beckons me. One of these days it may beckon me to my destruction. But I shall go with a smile, savouring the moment." He waited for no answering comment, but swept on, quickening his tone to a brisker pace. "We waste time, *citoyenne.* Listen, and afterwards resolve yourself. You will have time for thought between this and the event. Mistrust me, and remain to be presently guillotined; or trust me and let me lead you back to life. That shall be as you please. I offer; but I do not persuade. Listen now."

Swiftly, briefly he traced for her the course of events to come. He would procure the removal of the mental cases in the Archevêché, to a madhouse in the Rue du Bac, whence evasion would be easy. The removal would take place in the course of the next day. As soon as it was effected, he would depart for the Nivernais, being already commissioned by the Convention to undertake there a tour of inspection. His passports were ready, and they included a non-existent secretary. That was the place that she should fill, if she so decided, suitably dressed in man's attire for the purpose. Let her take time for thought, and let him know tomorrow, when he sought the house in the Rue du Bac, how she decided. He hoped that she would choose wisely. In the Nivernais she would be free to go her ways, and no doubt would know how to find shelter there in her native province and perhaps procure assistance to enable her to quit France should she so desire it. "We are Nivernais both," he ended by reminding her. "Perhaps it is compatriotism that strengthens my interest in you." He flashed a quick glance at the door, then, at last, swept off his hat, and bowed low. "My homage, *citoyenne.* I take my leave."

He was gone, abruptly, giving her no time to answer, leaving her there frowning in perplexity and buffeted between the fear of death and mistrust of her preserver.

That night from the height of the tribune in the hall of the Convention, Chauvinière inveighed furiously against the prison system, and the state of things he had found in the overcrowded prison hospital of the Archevêché. He was superb in his audacity, fulminating in his irony, which spared none of those responsible, nor hesitated to indict even the Minister of Justice, Camille Desmoulins. He claimed to speak in the name of Humanity, consumed by the fire of a just and righteous indignation.

A deputy from the lower Loire ventured to interrupt him with a gibe that drew some applause from the crowded assembly.

"Monsieur le President, will you permit this man to continue his monstrous advocacy of amenities for aristocrats?"

Chauvinière standing very straight, and looking very tall, his black head thrown back, his fine hands resting, one on either side of his plumed hat, on the ledge of the rostrum, stamped out at once the sparks of that spluttering applause.

"Aristocrats?" His voice broke about the heads of the deputies like a peal of thunder, and again: "Aristocrats?"

The silence was instantaneous. His indignant, questioning outcry had caught their attention. He paused now, and his sardonic imperious glance sought out that daring fellow from the Loire, and riveted him. He knew the value of suspense, and for a long moment he held them in it. Then he loosed his answer: "In a Nation of free men, Justice, citizens, should at once be inexorable, blind and undiscriminating. She can admit neither prejudice nor preconception, for these indeed are the negation of justice. In her divine eyes, which the ancients in their wisdom symbolically bandaged, there are neither aristocrats nor plebeians, but only accused. And lest Justice err in her findings – a danger revolting to enlightened men in this Age of Reason – she must presume the accused to be innocent until her own sifting of the evidence constrains her to convict them."

Applause rolled in volleys down that long hall. Chauvinière, who knew so well the power of words and how to wield them, knew also the value of dramatic poise. He remained now calm, precise, unmoved: the complete patriot with a duty to perform, who himself was nothing. No longer did his eyes seek out his erstwhile interrupter, lest he be suspected of gloating over the man's discomfiture. He did not even perceive – at least he did not return – the approving smile of the Deputy for Arras, that notorious humanitarian, the frail and livid Maximilian Robespierre, who removed one of the two pairs of glasses from his up-tilted nose, to beam upon the vehement tenant of the tribune.

After that the success of his advocacy was no longer in any doubt. His demand that as a commencement of reform the mental cases should instantly be removed from the Archevêché, so as to afford the sorely needed space for other sufferers was unanimously supported.

As he descended the steps of the tribune he reflected with cynical amusement that the blue-green eyes of Mademoiselle de Montsorbier were becoming responsible for internal politics in France. But there was, he also reflected, ample precedent in history from the days of one Helen, the shape of whose nose had brought about the siege of Troy.

Chapter Three

Dumey, the middle-aged physician who controlled the madhouse in the Rue du Bac, received a visit late in the afternoon of the following day from the Deputy Chauvinière. The deputy came in a travelling *chaise*, from which he removed a valise together with himself.

This he set down in the doctor's private room. He came straight to business in his peremptory, overbearing fashion.

"Among the demented prisoners entrusted to your care this morning is a *ci-devant*, a *Citoyenne* de Montsorbier."

"Ah yes!" The plump doctor's countenance became eager. "Her case—"

"Never mind her case. She is dead."

"Dead!" Dumey looked thunderstricken.

"Isn't that why you have sent for me?"

"Sent for you? But I didn't send for you."

"You are losing your memory, Dumey. Fortunately for both of us, I am not." His note was suddenly hard and faintly sinister, for all its eternal mockery. "You sent for me, as the nearest responsible member of the government, to assure myself of the decease, and countersign the death certificate which you are about to draw up and sign. My own signature will be witnessed by my secretary. He will appear presently. Now, pray conduct me to view the body."

Dumey looked at his visitor long and hard. There was that between them, on the subject of which a word from Chauvinière would send Dumey's head rolling into Sanson's basket: which was precisely why, of all the madhouses in Paris, Chauvinière had chosen this establishment in the Rue du Bac for the reception of the patients removed from the Archevêché. Against this danger on the one hand, Dumey had to set, on the other, favours received from the deputy and no doubt to be continued, one of which, indeed, was the present flow of patients to his house and his own consequent enrichment.

On both scores, whatever Chauvinière commanded, Dumey must perform. This even to the unquestioning risking of his head, since if he failed its removal was assured.

Dumey smiled at last his understanding and shrugged his resignation.

"The responsibility ..." He was beginning a little timidly.

"Will be mine, since I countersign your certificate. Hold your tongue, and no question of responsibility will ever arise. There will be no questions about any of your inmates for at least a month. When they come, you present your certificate. It will be too long after the event to admit of traces."

Dumey bowed, and conducted him. When he had unlocked the door of a room above-stairs, he would have led the way in, but the deputy arrested him.

"Wait outside, or, better still, go wait below in your room. You will the more easily forswear yourself if you do not see your patient again alive."

"But I shall have to see her. I—"

"You are mistaken. You will not. Go. Don't waste my time." Dumey departed. Chauvinière entered the room, carrying the valise.

Mademoiselle de Montsorbier, forewarned of his presence by his voice, was already standing to receive him. He bowed to her, deferentially, and this time he was so unrepublican as to remove his hat. Then he placed the valise on the table in mid-apartment.

"You have taken your resolve, *citoyenne?*" he said, between question and assertion. He had no doubt in his mind, this psychologist, that time and thought must have brought a person of her age to one conclusion only. It is very difficult to die willingly at twenty.

"I have resolved, monsieur," she answered him with quiet dignity.

"Citizen," he corrected her sharply. "There are very few monsieurs left in this country, and these are being guillotined so fast nowadays that presently there will be none at all. If you have resolved to live and to accept my good offices, *citoyenne,* you will oblige me by adopting at least the more obvious terms of our vocabulary of Liberty."

He had that preciseness of delivery which is so often the reflection of the ironical mind. Mademoiselle de Montsorbier began to discover in it a certain elusive quality of humour, but could not be sure whether this was conscious or unconscious, whether this member of the Convention was intentionally ironical or merely priggish, like so many of his colleagues.

She was scanning him closely now with those grave eyes of hers, seeking in his countenance an answer to her unspoken question.

He smiled as if he read her thought. "And you have resolved to live," he said. "That is very wise."

"I haven't said so." His penetration alarmed her a little.

"No? But I take so much for granted." He was apologetic. "I assume it from your calm, from the absence of defiance in your reception of me. It would desolate me to learn that I am mistaken."

"Mons—citizen, if I have misjudged you, I hope that you will have the generosity to forgive me. I—I hesitate to express myself upon your—your concern, your kindliness."

"Continue to hesitate. Expressions waste time, and we have none to spare." He threw open the valise. "Here, *citoyenne,* are the garments in which you will travel." He drew some of them forth. She recoiled, her face on fire.

"These! These! Impossible!"

"Oh, not impossible. Not at all impossible. A little difficult, perhaps. But I trust the difficulty will be overcome. If you will study the garments, the mystery of how they should be donned and worn will gradually vanish."

"That! But that is not the difficulty. You misunderstand me purposely."

"In the hope of making you perceive the absurdity of your qualms. My secretary cannot travel in a striped petticoat, and you will find these breeches … but there! We have no time to lose. I efface myself that you may make haste. When you are ready you will find me in the corridor."

A half-hour or so later, by when the deputy was in a ferment of impatience, a stripling figure, in round hat, black riding-coat, boots and breeches emerged from the lady's room. A moment Chauvinière detained her, to scrutinise her with an eye that missed no detail. Thus dressed she looked shorter by some inches, but her figure was well enough, and the queue of her hair had been cleverly contrived. He approved her in a word, and hurried her below. Dumey awaited them his certificate prepared. That business was soon over, and the Deputy Chauvinière, with his secretary closely following, entered the waiting *chaise*. Dumey closed the door upon them, and they were driven away.

No word passed between them until they were approaching the barrier, when Chauvinière handed his companion a bulky portfolio of black leather, partly opening it as he did so: "The passports are there on top. You will present them when they are demanded. It is in your office. No need to speak."

They drew up before the iron gates at the end of the Rue d'Enfer.

An officer in a blue coat with red woollen epaulettes (gold having been abolished as unbecoming an age of equality) pulled open the door and peremptorily challenged the travellers.

"Who goes there?"

It was Chauvinière who from his corner drawled the answer: "The Citizen-Deputy Chauvinière, Representative en Mission. Show him the papers, Antoine, and let us get on."

From under his lashes he watched his companion, ready to intervene at the first sign of blundering. But there was no such sign. Unfalteringly she took from the portfolio the papers he had designated, and proffered them with a hand that did not even tremble.

The officer, who had put aside a good deal of his peremptoriness upon learning with whom he had to deal, scanned the papers, returned them, saluted stiffly, and carefully reclosed the door. Then his voice rang out in command: "Pass the Citizen-Representative Chauvinière."

The iron gates creaked open, the driver cracked his whip, the guard presented arms and they rolled past the barrier and were out of Paris.

"We've crossed the Rubicon," said Chauvinière in his driest tone, and flung himself back in his corner, his long lean legs thrust straight before him. Thus reclining he furtively continued to observe his companion. She was composedly refolding the papers and replacing them in the portfolio. His wonder, his admiration, was so strong upon him that he uttered his thought aloud: "My faith! But you have spirit!"

She snapped the lock of the portfolio, and looked at him, smiling a little.

"It is in the blood," she said quietly. "You would not know that. Hence your surprise. You will not have known many women of my class, citizen-representative."

A lesser man would have been angered by the implication, which he was not fool enough to suppose was other than deliberate. But Chauvinière possessed that rare quality of detachment, which permitted him to admire deftness even when exercised to wound himself. He nodded his approval of her.

"I find you addicted to assumptions," he commented critically. "That, too, will be in the blood, and the cause of much of the shedding of it. Well, well! Let us talk of other things. My duties take me to Nevers. This is Thursday. We should be there by Saturday night. I don't spare horses when I travel on the business of the Nation."

She had already formed a suspicion of this from the furious pace at which the *chaise* was now being driven. The deputy continued: "What I propose for you is this." He paused, and in that pause she was conscious of a quickening of her pulses; a shortening of her breath. But Chauvinière watching her what time he deliberately tested her by this suspense, observed only her external unruffled calm. Slowly he proceeded: "Had you glanced at those passports you would have seen that their form is uncompromising. They command all, under pain of death, to afford us every assistance in their power on our travels in the prosecution of the Nation's business. When we reach Nevers, I shall discover that I require precise information of events in the extreme east of Burgundy. Too preoccupied with affairs in the Nivernais to go, myself, I shall decide to send you instead. For that purpose, and upon the authority of our passports, the Revolutionary Committee at Nevers shall supply you with the necessary safe-conduct, which will take you to the banks of the Rhone. After that, it will be for you – and you should not find it difficult – to discover means to cross into Switzerland, where you will be safe."

He ceased; but her breathing did not yet resume the normal. What she heard seemed utterly incredible. It clearly announced him to be acting from purely altruistic motives, with no thought of personal gain. Was it possible that her plight, or something in herself, had indeed moved him to this compassionate protection? Did such things happen, particularly at the hands of these human wolves who had made the revolution?

In consenting to take advantage of his offer, she had not permitted herself to be deceived by the specious terms in which it was made. She had accepted a desperate chance, who otherwise was lost. In accepting it, she had prepared herself to depend upon her own strength, courage and resource, to seize and use such opportunity as might offer to cheat him of any gain he might look to make for himself, to ensure as far as might be possible to her that he should perform as he seemed to promise.

Had she dishonoured him by these thoughts? Was this man, indeed, the selfless friend he protested himself, labouring for her salvation without hope of guerdon, as he had said? It seemed to her clear mind fantastic. Yet what else was to be assumed from the intentions he had just disclosed? Or was this merely a verbal opiate to lull her into a false confidence, so that she might lie the more utterly at his mercy?

Thus her thoughts in the long spell of silence that followed his announcement, until at last he broke again upon them, compelling speech.

"You are silent, *citoyenne*. You do not entirely approve of my dispositions? Or perhaps you have a better plan yourself?"

"No, no. It is not that." She paused to control the slight tremor in her voice. In the half-light of that interior it seemed to him that she had grown a little paler, as he considered the sweet profile with its finely drawn lip and delicately arched nose. "I am deeply moved, citizen, by your thought for me, which has gone so deep in planning, by the disinterested nobility of your concern."

His light eyes flickered. It was like the momentary upleaping and instant extinction of a flame in the dark. But she was not looking at him. She was staring straight before her.

"I have no words in which to thank you. I am dumb in my gratitude and wonder. Your plan for me seems everything I could desire. In Switzerland I have friends. I ..."

Her voice faltered and trailed into silence. It was no pretence that she was moved, that her self-control was slipping from her. She was daunted by the very need to command herself, to be alert, vigilant and ready for emergencies which might creep up to pounce upon her unawares. Her brave spirit, which might have preserved its vigour in the presence of revealed danger, was being battered down by uncertainty and suspense.

Chauvinière's voice, soft as silk, speaking on a sigh, penetrated the distraction of her mind.

"In that case, since you so completely approve, we may consider the matter decided, and act presently as I have said."

He settled himself back into his corner, closed his eyes, and thereafter for some three hours which that journey endured he seemed to doze. It was as if his interest in his travelling companion were already diminishing now that the intended service was already half-rendered and the remainder of it clearly plotted.

Chapter Four

They clattered over the kidney stones of Melun as dusk was falling and came to draw up at the Hotel de la Nation – lately the Hotel Royal. There, no sooner had a whisper gone forth from the postboy touching the identity of our traveller, than out came landlord, ostler and chamberlain to welcome him in trembling obsequiousness.

Chauvinière accepted this tribute to his greatness with a lofty disdain which few despots could have equalled, none surpassed. The best rooms were placed at the disposal of himself and his young secretary; the best supper Melun could provide was prepared for his august consumption; and a very choice old Burgundy was discovered in the cellar where it had lain neglected, and brought forth for the representative's delectation.

At table and thereafter his demeanour towards Mademoiselle de Montsorbier was of a correctness which could not have been exceeded by one of her own class. He was solicitous, but always deferential; kindly, but never lacking in respect. And he entertained her presently with talk which displayed unsuspected depths of culture, acquaintance not only with the works of Scarron and Voltaire, but also with the classical authors whom he freely quoted. His personality began to abash her a little, in a measure as she discovered it so greatly to transcend all that at first she had suspected. He displayed a refinement almost incredible in one of his political creed; his manners were impeccable.

When at last she retired for the night, she went in an uncertainty more profound than ever. He held the door for her, his head deferentially inclined, and with a courteously expressed wish for her good repose. Within her room, which was next to his own, a wave of panic suddenly swept over her. She drove home the bolts with which her door was furnished at base and summit, then went to open her window, so as to ascertain what line of retreat might be available in case of need. It was cold and drizzling and the night was overcast and very dark. But light from a ground-floor window showed her the gleaming cobbles of the yard, a good fifteen feet below. At need with a twisted sheet she might go that way. But what then? Such a course was only to be contemplated in desperate case, and her case was not yet desperate. Indeed, she sought to assure herself, she had no cause to consider it desperate at all. She was a little coward, shuddering at shadows.

She was even more strongly of this opinion when she awakened in the morning, refreshed by unbroken sleep, the spring sunshine flooding her little white room, and realised on awakening how needlessly imagination had made a craven of her.

She came spruce and trim to breakfast, so spruce and trim that a serving-maid in the corridor gazed with a shy smile at the citizen-representative's young secretary, and may have been distressed by that austere young man's indifference to her charms.

Chauvinière was already at table. As there was a servant in the room, he did not rise. He nodded curtly, and his greeting had an edge.

"Ah, Antoine! You slept well, I trust?"

"Excellently, I thank you, citizen-representative."

"In future do not sleep quite so well, if you please. I dislike late-comers and young men who are reluctant to leave their beds. Your breakfast is cold, and the horses are already being harnessed. We set out in ten minutes. See that you are ready."

They travelled all that day at a furious rate, and with but two halts for food and rest and change of horses, so that before nightfall they had gone sixty miles and came to rest at Châtillon sur Laing, a village of the Orléannais. Here the experience of the previous night was repeated. Again Chauvinière observed a deference that was almost exaggerated, again he talked glibly and entertainingly, displaying, as it were, all the jewels of his mind to dazzle and beglamour her. She thawed a little. Indeed, it was impossible to remain frozen in aloofness under the glow of so much benignity. Yet once or twice, looking up suddenly, she caught his eyes upon her. They shifted instantly, and the wolfish expression she surprised upon his face was as instantly covered as if by a mask. But the impression of it remained upon her memory, to evoke a sudden ineffable dread, akin to that with which his eyes had smitten her in the Conciergerie.

He drank perhaps too much that evening, and in consequence slackened a little the reins of his self-control. For in holding the door for her departure and in wishing her good night, the leer on his lace and the hungry glow of his eyes were unmistakable. Such was the fear they roused in her, that having locked and bolted her door, she flung herself fully dressed upon her bed, her mind in such a state of vigilance, that she scarcely slept at all until the dawn. Yet nothing happened to justify her tremors of spirit, and when she came to breakfast she found herself awaited by a representative so correct and formal in his manner that she asked herself whether again her imagination had not tricked her on the previous night.

All day that question abode with her, whilst the *chaise* swayed and rocked in its headlong speed and Chauvinière half-dozed in his corner with a disregard of her that was almost ungallant. It was still with her when at five o'clock in the afternoon within a half-mile of La Charité, a village on the Loire, their journey came to a sudden lurching end as the result of the loss of an axle-pin, which, but for the postboy's quick perception, might have had more serious consequences.

Chauvinière climbed down, swearing savagely. It had been his purpose to reach Nevers that night, there to address a meeting of the Committee of Public Safety and so to plan that upon the morrow he might set out upon his survey. That plan he must now abandon, and accept such a kennel as La Charité could offer his republican sybaritism.

Yet when they had tramped the half-mile of muddy road to the village, they found there an excellent inn, where they were given a good room above-stairs in which to sup, with a bedroom opening from each side of it. Within an hour of their arrival an unusually good supper was placed before them by the vintner and his comely wife, who did not spare themselves in their endeavour to earn the commendation of the great man from Paris by whom, in their own words, their poor house was honoured.

Over the well-larded capon Chauvinière expressed himself to his secretary.

"By this I should judge that there is a good deal of aristocracy surviving in this Nivernais of yours."

"You should be thankful for that since it provides you with so good a supper."

"In this world, as you may come to find, the greater the cause for thankfulness on the one hand, the greater the cause for repining on the other. It is thus that Fortune bestows her favours: taking payment always."

"The payment of a debt is no good cause for repining," she objected.

He looked at her, so intently, so inscrutably, that all her fears of yesterday evening suddenly returned, and she shivered. He observed it.

"You are cold," he said, and she fancied that the shadow of a smile swept almost imperceptibly across his lean face. "Let me close the window." He rose, and crossed the room; and it was whilst he stood with his back towards her, humouring the catch of the lattice, that she suddenly took her resolve to end this suspense, to put his intentions regarding her to an immediate test. And her fertile mind at once supplied the necessary elements. She waited only until he had returned to the table.

"You have been very good to me, incredibly good to me, citizen."

He paused to stare at her, his hand upon the back of the tilted chair.

"What need to speak of that?"

Her eyes were upon the coarsely woven tablecloth; between finger and thumb she was kneading a little ball of crumb.

"I must speak of it because the time has come to thank you; to thank you, and to part."

She looked up suddenly to surprise his expression and found it compounded of suspicion, anger and dismay.

"Part?" He frowned as he uttered the word. With heightened incredulity he repeated: "Part?"

She explained herself. "We are already in the Nivernais. It is my own country. I have friends throughout the province—"

"Friends? What friends?" His tone suggested that their mention should be their death warrant.

"I will not name them lest I compromise them. That would not be fair to them, nor indeed, quite fair to you. It might test your duty too severely. Neither would it be fair to you that I accompany you into Nevers in broad daylight tomorrow. After all, I was well-known there not so many months ago. There will be many left who might recognise me. Seeing me in your company and thus, what could they assume? You would be compromised, and—"

"Compromised!" His scornful laughter shook the crazy windows. "And who in Nevers would dare to compromise me?"

She smiled upon him rather wistfully, slowly nodding her fair head. "You are of a high courage, citizen; of a reckless audacity, as I have observed. But I will not permit you to add to the heavy debt under which already I lie, the risk perhaps of your life …"

"Tush! No more of that, *citoyenne!* I run no risk. But if I did, what then? My life is my own to risk as I choose, and not as you or any other presumes to permit. We are free men all in this reformed France." His tone resumed its habitual sardonic note. "And we need no permission for our acts. All that went with the days of tyranny."

"Your generosity cannot deceive me." Her blue-green eyes looked at him resolutely. "And that is why we part tonight."

He leaned forward across the board. His face was very grave. It had lost, or seemed to have lost, some of its habitual colour.

"You give me news, *citoyenne*. We part tonight, eh? Tonight? So, so! And will you tell me where you are going?"

"I could not tell you that without compromising others."

He laughed. "You'll compromise the whole Nivernais before ever I let you go." The tone was fierce, snarling, as a dog snarls over a bone that is being wrested away. But immediately almost he had checked that too-revealing note. His voice was smooth again. "I mean, before I let you risk yourself in such a fashion. You'll forgive my insistence, *citoyenne*. But I have not jeopardised my neck to save yours from the guillotine just to have you throw my gift away in sheer wantonness. Oh no. I shall make sure of your safety before I part with you." He sat down at last.

"But you said in Paris—"

"Never mind what I said in Paris." There was an angry rumble in his voice. Again it was the note of the dog about to be robbed of the bone he had looked forward to enjoying. "Consider only what I have said here. I do not part with you until I am assured of your safety."

She sat there facing him across the board with terror in her heart, her eyes dilating a little as they met now his smouldering glance, observed the flush on his prominent cheek bones and the scowl on that lofty brow across which a clump of his moist black hair had fallen like a curtain.

She was answered. Her suspense at least, her doubts and questionings were at an end. He was the wolf she had at first supposed him, and she was the prey he promised himself. Why, she wondered, did he stalk her so warily and patiently? It was not hers to understand the man's sybaritic fastidiousness which rendered repugnant to him the notion of prevailing without real conquest.

Of her terror she permitted him to catch no glimpse. All that was disclosed to him by her rigid stare was surprise. Then the surprise passed, chased away by a smile, a smile of a sweetness and gentleness such as she had never yet vouchsafed him. She averted her eyes.

"Your generosity … your nobility leaves me without words. You bring me almost to tears, citizen; tears of gratitude. And yet—"

"Add nothing more," he implored her. His voice grew hoarse. "You have yet to learn the depth of a devotion which would stop at nothing in your service, Cléonie."

One of his long arms came across the table, and his fine hand closed upon hers where it lay there beside her plate. A moment she let it remain, loathing his touch, repressing the shudder that might betray this loathing, and loathing herself for the duplicity to which circumstances compelled her to descend. Then, hot with a shame, whose flush he entirely misunderstood, smiling with a rather piteous wistfulness she gently disengaged her hand and rose.

"Suffer me to go," she begged him. "I—I am a little confused."

"No! Wait!" He too, had risen, and stood eager beyond the dividing board, to him so inopportunely placed.

"Tomorrow!" she begged him faintly. "We will talk again tomorrow, citizen. Let me go now! Ah, let me go!"

Almost she overdid it, almost she overacted the suggestion of a spiritual struggle against the magnetism of his personality. With another, indeed, it might have been entirely fatal. But Chauvinière the psychologist knew the full value of restraint, knew how much more complete is the ultimate surrender to a generous opponent. He bowed low in silence save for a little sigh, and by the time he came upright again he was alone. She had slipped like a ghost into the adjacent room. He saw the white door close. He heard the bolts rasp home. He smiled as he stood there. Then he sighed again, still smiling, resumed his chair and poured himself wine.

Behind her bolted door Mademoiselle de Montsorbier stood breathless and a little faint. She leaned against it, listening to his movements, and gradually she resumed her self-command.

She crossed at last to the dressing-table, and by the dim light of the single candle burning there surveyed her face. She accused it of pallor, assured herself that there was nothing to be feared, then drawing up a chair, sat down before her mirror, but made no attempt to prepare herself for bed.

Thus for a half-hour, at the end of which she heard the rasp of his chair in the outer room, followed by the sound of his pacing to and fro like a caged animal. Once his steps came right up to her door and paused there. She stiffened. She was conscious of the roughening of her skin, of the acceleration of her pulses as she waited through that pause, which seemed interminable, waited for his knock. It came at last, sharply rapped, and the sound brought her to her feet.

By a miracle she kept her voice steady. "Who is there?"

"It is I, *citoyenne;* Chauvinière."

"What do you want, *citoyen*?"

There was a long pause before his answer came: "To warn you, that we set out early in the morning. The *chaise* will be ready at eight o'clock."

"I shall be punctual, *citoyen*. Good night!"

"Good night, *citoyenne.*"

His footsteps receded. Scarcely crediting her ears she listened to them as they crossed the length of the outer room. Then she heard him pass into his own chamber, and at last came the closing of his door. She was able to breathe again. But it was in vain that she sought to explain that trivial incident. Had he deliberately sought to scare her, merely so as to show that all fear of him was idle and thus lull her into a sense of false security, or had his action been genuine?

She crossed the room and flung herself upon the bed, fully dressed as she was, even to her riding-boots, but she left the candle burning and made no attempt to go to sleep.

With a patience and self-control that were miraculous considering what was in her mind, she lay thus, listening and waiting for a full two hours until she could be sure that the house slept. Then, at last, she rose, and removed her boots. She took up the guttering candle, and very softly withdrew the bolts of her door. Cautiously, soundlessly, she opened it, and soundlessly crept out into the room beyond, which now was all in darkness. A moment she paused, listening. From beyond the far door came a sound of mild snoring. The citizen-representative was asleep.

With her boots in one hand and the candle held aloft in the other she tiptoed towards the door that opened to the stairs. Midway across the room she checked. Something gleamed lividly on a side table and drew her glance. It was the clasp of the representative's portfolio. She paused, hesitating, scared by the temptation that assailed her, to which at last, with a pale smile, she yielded. She snatched up the portfolio and tucked it under her arm. Then she passed out, and in her stockinged feet cautiously descended the creaking staircase.

In the passage below she paused to put on her boots. Then very carefully she drew the bolts of a side door, and stepped out into the stable yard. Here a shock awaited her. Although it was past midnight, a light showed in the stables; the upper half of the stable door stood open, and above the closed lower half she beheld the bust of a man who leaned there, who had observed her exit, and who now straightened himself to challenge her. Instantly resolved, she forestalled him.

"Ah! You are astir! It is fortunate, for otherwise I must have fetched you from your bed. I need a horse at once, citizen."

"A horse? Name of a name! A horse at this hour?"

"Business of the Nation." The young secretary's voice was hard and peremptory. He flourished his portfolio. "I am to ride ahead of the citizen-representative into Nevers. There is urgency. Make haste, or you will answer to the citizen-representative."

The ostler asked no more questions. A horse was quickly saddled, and upon this the young secretary, with a seat suggestive of a huntsman rather than a clerk, vanished at the gallop into the night.

Chapter Five

The citizen-representative, newly risen, scrupulously shaved, his hair dressed as carefully as an aristocrat's, stalked into the main room between the bedrooms, calling briskly for chocolate.

Whilst he waited he sauntered to the window, and stood there considering the greyness and drizzle of that melancholy March morning. Presently, however, the general stillness about him smote his attention as a sudden sound might have done at another time. He cocked his head, listened for some movement from Mademoiselle de Montsorbier's room. The unbroken silence moved him apprehensively. He stepped swiftly to the door and rapped sharply with his knuckles. There was no answer. He tried the handle. It turned, and the door swung inwards, discovering to him the room's lack of tenant. He crossed the threshold, and gazed about him frowning. He noted the bed, undisturbed save by an impression of her form so faint as to suggest that it was some hours since she had lain there, nor then had lain there long.

He stepped back, his face dark, his square chin thrust forward. His eyes sought the side table on which, as he remembered, he had too carelessly and trustingly left his portfolio. It was no longer there, which was already as he had expected. A moment yet he paused to make sure that it was not elsewhere. Then, with an oath, he flung headlong from the room, crashing into the serving-maid who was bearing him his chocolate. Her scream and the clattering smash of the scattered chocolate service followed him as he bounded down the stairs, bawling for the innkeeper.

The innkeeper, terrified by the representative's torrential descent and tempestuous demands for his secretary, backed by horrible threats of the guillotine in the event of prevarication or evasion, quaveringly swore by the God of the Old Regime and the Goddess of Reason of the New, that he knew nothing whatever of the missing person and that he learnt now for the first time of that person's absence. But the ostler, lounging near at hand and overhearing the angry interrogatory, came forward to supply the answer which was to quench Chauvinière's last lingering hope.

The citizen-representative stared at the mumbling oaf with such fierce flaming eyes that the fellow recoiled in dread.

"And you let him go?" said Chauvinière between his teeth. He was smiling terribly. "You let him go? Like that?"

"How should I have known that—"

"How should you know anything, animal? Brute beast, did it not occur to you that an honest man doesn't sneak away like a thief at midnight?" He smothered him in obscene epithets, cuffed him in his overpowering rage, and when the fellow protested against such treatment in the name of Liberty, Equality and Fraternity, cuffed him again more soundly.

"Will you raise your voice to me, carrion? If you must be talking, tell me at least which way he went. Use your worthless head, animal, or you may lose it over this."

The ostler answered at random that the youth had ridden off in the direction of Nevers.

At last Chauvinière controlled himself.

"Saddle me a horse," he commanded, and on that horse he was, himself riding away to Nevers within ten minutes, leaving the postboy to follow with the *chaise*.

He rode at a pace which reflected the fury of his mind. More even than the loss of the girl did it enrage him to think that a man of his wit and acumen should have permitted that smoothly spoken, lying little aristocrat to have cheated him last night with her simpering pretence of yielding weakness, thereby fooling him into an exercise of idiotic patience so as to render his conquest ultimately more complete. He was rightly served for his imbecile forbearance. But when he found her, as find her he would though he destroyed a province in the search, she should mercilessly be taught what it meant to play comedy with the emotions of such a man.

He was very much the wolf that morning, the wolf questing for the lamb that has eluded him and licking his chops in anticipation of the voracious unsparing feast to come when that lamb shall eventually have been overtaken and reduced into possession.

He paused at Rougues to munch a crust and drink a glass of brandy and water – for he had ridden away fasting from La Charité – then spurred on again, reaching Nevers at noon.

He went straight to the President of the Revolutionary Committee of Nevers, a heavy-bodied lumbering tanner named Desjardins, and stated his immediate need. His papers had been stolen last night at La Charité by a youth whom he had befriended, and whom he was now assured was a girl, a cursed aristocrat, no doubt. She was known to have ridden off in the direction of Nevers. She might attempt to pass herself off as Chauvinière's secretary. Her recapture was of the utmost importance. Heads would fall if she were not retaken. Chauvinière would see to that. Desjardins was summoned to assemble at once the agents of the Committee of Safety, to inform them of the case, and to stimulate them to track down the thief.

"And they had better be active," swore Chauvinière, "or, by Saint Guillotine, I'll give them a lesson in zeal!"

With that, the representative who was half-famished, went off to dine at the Auberge du Soleil, whither the *chaise* had been ordered to follow.

That the agents of the Committee were active is not to be doubted. In fact their activities were proved by the recapture on the morrow, near Chatillon, of the horse which the girl had ridden, and, later, by the discovery in a ditch near Souvigny of a black riding-coat, boots and other articles of apparel which Chauvinière recognised as those worn by the fugitive, as well as of an empty portfolio of black leather with a metal clasp, which the representative acknowledged for his own stolen property. Of the fugitive herself however, there was no trace. The agents inclined to the convenient belief that she was dead, and pointed to the clothes as evidence.

Chauvinière withered them with his contempt. "Women do not undress themselves to die by the roadside, you imbeciles! Continue the search. It will be rendered more difficult by the fact that she has changed her apparel. But continue it. Put yourselves on the track of any stranger of whom you may hear. Strangers do not move unperceived in country districts. Display your zeal."

They returned to their quest, shrugging and grumbling among themselves and confiding in one another that the citizen-representative was an obstinate pig of a mule, an arrogant bully who gave himself the airs of an aristocrat and who would come to an evil end.

Days were added to those already spent, until their tale made up a week, during which Chauvinière sat brooding at the Sign of the Sun, snarling ill-humouredly at all who sought him, and giving, apparently, no thought to the affairs of the Convention which were responsible for his visit to the Nivernais. When reminded of this by the greatly daring Desjardins, he first stormed at the audacity of the reminder, then swore profusely by the new gods and the old that the Nivernais should know of his presence. With that oath he took up his neglected duties, conquering his infatuation and vain regrets, and putting Mademoiselle de Montsorbier, at least for the present, from his mind.

And as he had wrathfully promised he performed. In that month of April the Nivernais came to shudder at the name of a man who, whatever he may have been in the past, had never been wanton or crude in his cruelties and never bloodthirsty. From township to township he swept with the horrible paraphernalia of his justiciary's office at his heels, and ruthlessly practised in bloodshed the doctrines of the new Golden Age of Reason.

Throughout the Nivernais the revolutionary movement had been conducted upon moderate lines. Therefore was there the more work for such a man in such a mood, and the more terrifying did that work appear to the inhabitants.

At last towards the end of April his dread progress brought him to the little hill town of Poussignot. If it had trembled at the news of his approach, it was almost prostrated with terror at the manner of his descent upon it. A military guard of honour escorted the travelling *chaise* in which he lounged in his grey coat, plumed hat and sash of office. In the wake of his carriage trailed a cart laden with baulks and beams of scarlet-painted timber, presently to be assembled into a guillotine and mounted in the market square. Upon the cart's grim load sat an obese, dull-eyed, phlegmatic man, the sight of whom sent a shudder through those who guessed his office. With him was an equally obese woman, blear-eyed, unkempt and slatternly, who drove the cart.

The Revolutionary Committee of Poussignot, which had been duly elected upon representations from Nevers a year ago, but which had never yet found occasion to function, was hurriedly summoned to assemble in the little town hall, overlooking the market square, where the carpenters were already busy with the erection of the scaffold. In muttering awe they awaited the coming of this dread man from the Convention, who was to rouse that sleepy and hitherto contented township from its revolutionary languor.

He kept them waiting a full hour while he dined, careless of the time he thus wantonly wasted for them. He arrived at last, arrogant and overbearing in manner, arrogant and cruelly sardonic in speech. He found here in Poussignot a state of things which supplied ample material for the mockery which was never very distant from his outlook. Whilst France herself was clattering into ruin under the revolutionary earthquake that shook her from end to end, Poussignot, in the very heart of France, appeared to have gone to sleep, and in its state of incredible somnolence to have pursued the peaceful even tenor of the days of the abominable ancient regime. It was so incredible that after the first shock of surprise, Chauvinière was moved to inward laughter: laughter at the sleeper and at the thought of the awakening in store.

The many activities that had engaged his mind during the past month had gradually dimmed the memory of Mademoiselle de

Montsorbier, and his chagrin at the manner in which she had victimised him. In a measure as her image faded, so too had faded gradually the savage humour which that memory had inspired and which he had vented upon all and sundry. It was fortunate for Poussignot that by the time he reached it, he was growing nauseated by bloodshed and weary of the crude pursuit of victims for the knife. The more normal attitude of philosophy upon which he secretly prided himself was gradually returning. His sense of humour was gradually reasserting itself. Poussignot restored it to him completely, although the overawed Committee, now listening to his passionate tirade, was permitted no glimpse of this.

In his deep, vibrant voice, pitched on a note of stinging sarcasm, he trounced that Revolutionary Committee, upbraiding the supineness of its members, threatening them with the doom they had been so reluctant to dispense unto others, unless he beheld them more zealous in the sacred service of Liberty.

Having thoroughly startled them out of their complacency, having delivered them a sermon upon the new gospel of Equality which he gathered was insufficiently understood in the hills of Poussignot, and having impressed them with the necessity of extirpating all those who were heretical or lukewarm or otherwise a danger to the spread of the glorious new religion, he passed from the general to the particular.

He came already informed, it appeared, of certain things in and about Poussignot, and he now produced a list of persons suspected of the new crime of incivisme, in one or another of its many forms.

"This list I am about to read to you; and I invite your serious consideration of the persons whose names you are to hear. For you are not to suppose ..." And here he broke off to swing half-round towards the window which overlooked the square where the scarlet guillotine was in course of erection. To indicate it to them, he flung out an arm in a gesture supremely dramatic. "You are not to suppose that engine, that noble glaive of Freedom, that glorious scythe of Equality, under which the heads of the despots and the privileged have been shorn away, is being erected there merely as an idle ornament to your town."

They trembled, never suspecting that this terrible jester indulged his perverted sense of humour by making a mock for his own secret amusement of the very gospel which he was sent to preach. There were moments when Chauvinière appeared almost to be probing the ignoble depths to which men may be reduced by terror. More than once had he startled his brethren in the Convention itself by solemn fulminations in which it was almost impossible not to suspect sarcasm, yet of which none would have dared to voice that suspicion. One of these moments was upon him now. Inwardly his warped soul was writhing with gleeful laughter at the psychological humours of the situation he created by the images he evoked.

"I must not be understood to say that such an engine would be an idle ornament in any town, even if a virtuous republicanism, too general to be hoped, should compel it to stand idle. For, ask yourselves, my friends, my brothers, what statue of ignoble King, of wretched tyrant, or vile servant of despotism, what image of snivelling saint or mouldering so-called martyr, could ever compare with that glorious symbol of Man's Emancipation, of Man's Deliverance from the fetters that were placed by Kings and Priests upon his very soul. There it rises, my brothers, in its awful dignity, the emblem of the Triumph of Reason. And what more glorious emblem could any city desire to raise. That scaffold, my brethren, is a sacred altar, upon which it is your holy duty to offer up the impure blood of aristocrats to the greater honour and glory of the Republic, One and Indivisible!"

Under his fiery eyes they huddled together like a flock of terrified sheep. He observed them calmly.

"You are silent, my friends. I understand. You share my own deep emotion. It leaves you speechless in your great thankfulness. That is very well. It is a sign to me that you will not falter in the performance of the exalted duties of the office to which you have had the honour to be elected by the voice of the people, which is the voice of the gods." He raised the list which his left hand had held throughout the exordium, and his tone sank quietly from its lofty note of exaltation. "Let us come now to practical, to precise considerations. Let me read you these names and the crimes of which their bearers are suspected."

There were men on his list whom he charged with being friendly with despots, others with being so closely related to *émigrés* that their own *civisme* must be in doubt until thoroughly tested; others whom he understood to be in league with reactionaries in other parts of France; others who were thought to be in correspondence with the enemies of France beyond her frontiers; and there were others he named as ripe for revolutionary justice on the score of birth alone.

It was upon naming the third of these last – one Raoul Amédée Corbigny de Corbal – that he received his first check.

"Of what is he accused, that one?"

The question came abruptly from Doucier, the horse-leech, a man prominent in the local Jacobin Society, and President of the Revolutionary Committee; a passionate but entirely academic republican, who was honest, fearless and formidable in debate, a man who might, had he so chosen, have represented his own section of the Nivernais in the National Convention. He was the first, as might have been expected, to throw off the spell of terror which Chauvinière had imposed upon the Committee, and to shake himself free of the net of words in which the representative had caught and held them.

The emissary of the Convention was aghast at the audacious interruption. He answered it impatiently: "He is accused of incivisme."

"But in what form?" Doucier insisted.

"Form?" Chauvinière frowned upon him. The question was inconvenient. He shrugged. "In the form of harbouring counter-revolutionary sentiments." It was the best that he could do, and it should suffice.

Doucier, however, proved of a disconcerting appetite for detail. He gathered courage as he went and in a measure as he perceived that his questions discomposed the great man from Paris.

"What expression is it alleged that the Citizen Corbal has given to these sentiments?"

"Expression!" Chauvinière's rich voice was almost shrill. "Name of God! Do you take the risk of defending him?"

"When I hear precisely of what he is accused, I may consider the necessity."

"But I've told you already … Name of a name!"

"Not precisely, citizen-representative. Not precisely. And the Committee of Poussignot demands precise accusations; not vague charges which of its own knowledge it perceives to be unfounded."

An approving growl from the assembly informed Chauvinière that infected by the example of their President the members of the Committee had so far recovered from the spell of his oratory as to be in a state of mutiny.

"Do you say that I lie?" he asked them icily.

"Oh! But, citizen-representative! Only that you may have been misinformed. Unable to compile your list from personal knowledge, we realise that you must have received assistance and advice. We realise also, when we find in your list the name of one who is generally esteemed, who is known to all for a true republican at heart—"

Chauvinière interrupted violently. "A true republican at heart! What next! What cant do you dare to offer me? You had better look to your own heads, my friends, if you have learnt your duties no better than to see a true republican in a pestilential *ci-devant* aristocrat."

But Doucier was too well-informed to accept this as conclusive.

"The two are not inconsistent. You could say the same of the Marquis de Mirabeau, without whom there might have been no revolution. If you will suffer us to guide you in matters of local knowledge, citizen, you will accept our assurance that you have been not only misled, but deliberately misled, by counsellors whose aims are perhaps reactionary. I assure you, citizen, that the gravest consequences might follow upon an unsubstantiated attack upon Corbigny de Corbal. In Poussignot all the world knows the stalwart and practical republicanism of his principles; all the world knows the unpretentious simplicity of his existence, and all the world loves him. That is not a man to be lightly accused. For your own sake, citizen-representative, and for ours, you would do well to be fully armed with particulars of Corbal's incivisme before you demand of us his arrest and trial."

If the argument did not suffice to turn Chauvinière from his purpose, at least it sufficed to make him temporise.

He announced that he would pay a visit to Corbal, and form at first hand an opinion of the real sentiments of the *ci-devant* Vicomte.

Thereupon he proceeded with his list, which for the rest was mainly concerned with priests who had declined to take the constitutional oath, with others who having taken it, yet refused or neglected to adopt the constitutional forms of worship, and with others still who whilst conforming to all prescriptions, yet rendered themselves suspect of insincerity by their persistent celibacy. And when Doucier ventured the opinion that this was too slender a ground for suspicion, he launched Chauvinière upon one of his sinister excursions in comic philosophy.

"Celibacy," the representative announced, "is an affront to Nature, and who affronts Nature affronts republicanism, which is based on Natures laws."

And upon that, catching fire from his own sententiousness, he reverted to his earlier truculence and invective. He charged them with lukewarmness where the interests of the Nation were concerned, and warned them not to throw obstacles in the path of his sacred duly, which was to uproot from the holy soil of Republican France the last seed of incivisme which sapped the nourishment required by the noble tree of Liberty, planted by the hand of Reason and fertilised by the blood of patriots. He closed upon a rhetorical exhortation, much in the same manner, that they should not compel him to report to the Executive in Paris that he found the Revolutionary Committee of Poussignot supine, lethargic and tainted with reactionary sentiments.

On that, perceiving that by his manner and perfervid oratory he had reconquered much of the ground momentarily lost, he abruptly and dramatically withdrew.

Of the truth of their warning about Corbigny de Corbal, of the esteem and affection in which the man was held, he sought and presently found abundant confirmation in the town. This irritated him, unreasonably perhaps. That such a thing could be at such a time showed him how profound was the somnolence of Poussignot, how deep a sense of complacency this little township of the Nivernais permitted itself. All his life Chauvinière had detested complacency. Taking, like an intelligent man, no satisfaction in himself, he loathed the spectacle of self-satisfaction in others, and sought to smash it wherever he met it. He would smash it here in Poussignot in its most confident expression, namely, in the *ci-devant* Vicomte de Corbal. If civisme, as then understood, was so wide a thing that Corbal could sit comfortable and secure within it, then it remained for Chauvinière to discover how to narrow civisme down to Corbal's exclusion. But because he did not wish to set counter-revolutionary fires alight under his feet, he went about the business with prudence. And he began his study of the problem by paying a visit to Corbal.

Chapter Six

The Chateau de Corbal was a solid, unpretentious mansion, perched amid vineyards halfway up the hill above the town, standing four-square, grey and a little dilapidated, flanked by round towers under red extinguisher roofs.

Within doors, the citizen-representative found the same solid unpretentiousness, stressed by faded decorations, which should long since have been renewed, and shabby furnishings, much of which should long since have been burned. That this unpretentiousness extended to Corbal's mode of life was evident when Chauvinière, conducted to the vast stone kitchen, found him there at table with the persons of his household, whom he simply described as his "family." They consisted of his elderly steward, Fougereot, the latter's wife, and their two stalwart sons and a plump comely young woman euphoniously named Filomene, who was responsible for the domestic comforts of the impoverished nobleman. Corbal himself, a man of thirty, fitted into his environment as if expressly designed for it. In dress he was almost a peasant, in dignity and in general bearing a gentleman, whilst in speech and in countenance, with his lofty brow and sombre wistful eyes, he suggested the scholar and the poet.

Born to an impoverished estate, he had accommodated himself without idle repining. He had never been to Court, or served his King in any capacity; but from early adolescence he had devoted himself to the cultivation of his three or four hundred acres, directing and in time of need even personally assisting in sowing and reaping, in crushing his own wine and oil and in threshing his own corn like the humblest *métayer.*

When the monarchy fell with the leaves in the autumn of '92, it was said in his reproach by men of his class that he was of those who had done nothing to uphold it, which was quite true. For when feudalism lay agonising and a party of neighbouring noblemen came to summon him to his duty as they conceived it, to exhort him to rally to his King, Monsieur Corbigny de Corbal had epitomised his political faith in his reply: "Messieurs, the King is in no danger unless it be that which you may create for him. By resisting a nation's just demands, you rush upon destruction. By identifying the throne with your resistance, you will destroy the throne with yourselves."

These words, being widely reported, increased the respect and affection in which he was held in the countryside. It was not for nothing that nature had given him those eyes, rendered wistful by what they found in the heart of things, to which their glances penetrated.

He rose now to receive his visitor, with a dignified deference in which there was no trace of that uneasiness discernible in the members of his household. He was of a good height and finely made, and his self-command and courtliness were of the kind that compel courtesy in return from all save the hopelessly boorish. Chauvinière was not of these, and therefore he came, a little to his own astonishment, under the spell of the *ci-devant's* ingratiating personality.

"You take me by surprise, citizen," Corbal apologised. "It is not so unceremoniously that I should wish to receive a representative of the government."

"I represent a government, citizen, that dispenses with ceremony," Chauvinière replied, but with a good deal less than his usual haughty sententiousness.

"No government should ever quite do that." Corbal's singularly sweet smile disarmed any resentment which his disagreement might provoke. "Governments are set up to govern; to govern successfully they must inspire respect, and ceremony is the natural expression of respect. Men are not humbled by deference to those things which in themselves command it. On the contrary, they are dignified."

Chauvinière raised his brows despite himself. Was the ci-devant, he wondered, permitting himself some of that covert ironic humour in which the representative dealt so freely and with such secret relish?

"A philosopher!" he said, and was not quite innocent of a sneer.

"That is too big a word to describe me, citizen. I have lived long alone; and so I have studied a good deal, to combat loneliness. But I keep you standing. Will you not join our board?" He placed a chair. "You will find us of a republican simplicity."

"That is as it should be," said Chauvinière, who detested republican simplicity, and daily thanked God for a revolution which had brought the succulent things of life within his easy reach. He sat down. He was served by Filomene with bread and ham, both of which he found of an excellent quality, whilst Corbal himself poured for him a wine which left little to be desired. Not so impossibly republican, after all, this simple fare.

Corbal resumed his seat. "I am honoured, citizen-representative, my poor house is honoured, by the visit of so illustrious a member of the Convention."

Again a suspicion that he was being mocked crossed Chauvinière's mind. His piercing eyes were upon the *ci-devant*. "And you are not at all inquisitive as to its occasion?"

Corbal smiled, completely at ease. "You are my guest, citizen. It is not for me to pester you with questions. In your own good time you shall tell me in what I may have the honour of serving you."

"You are of a gratifying patience," Chauvinière commended him, and gave his attention to the ham.

Thereafter Corbal and his odd guest chatted desultorily of this and that, whilst the others sat listening in uneasy silence. At length, the meal being ended, Chauvinière sat back, Hung one buckskinned leg over the arm of his chair and tucked his long hand under the tricolour sash of office that girdled him: a man taking his ease familiarly.

"You are very snug here at Corbal, citizen. I wonder that you have never brought a mistress to it."

It was an idle sentence, uttered to break fresh conversational ground. Filomene was standing behind Corbal's chair at the moment, squarely facing Chauvinière. The sudden flicker of her eyelids, the little spasm of pain that rippled across her plump, comely face to be instantly suppressed did not escape the watchful eye of the representative, and may have inspired the impish notion of how this elusive *ci-devant* might well be hobbled.

Monsieur Corbigny de Corbal laughed; but it was a laugh in which Chauvinière caught more wistfulness than mirth.

"What would you? I have waited perhaps too long. In earlier life I wooed the land too assiduously. Today …" he shrugged. "Today it would be not easy perhaps to find …" He checked abruptly, as one checks on the brink of an indiscretion.

But the indiscretion was committed; Chauvinière had no difficulty in completing the *ci-devant's* sentence. He had meant to say that it was not easy to find a woman of his own class in a France which had been purged of aristocrats.

"To find what, citizen?" he coaxed.

"Oh, but nothing, citizen." Corbal was faintly embarrassed. "It does not matter. And it would be easy to discover a more interesting topic of conversation than myself."

"You are mistaken in both opinions. It matters very much. And it is precisely to talk of yourself that I am here."

"You desire to flatter me, citizen?"

Chauvinière's last doubt was now removed that the fellow had the audacity secretly to laugh at him. But he let it pass. He had thought of something else. The sentence with which he had rebuked the Revolutionary Committee of Poussignot suddenly recurred to him, and he served it up to his host.

"Celibacy is an affront to Nature; and who affronts Nature is no good republican, since republicanism is based on Nature's laws. That is why I say that it matters very much."

They did not take him seriously. Old Fougereot led the laugh in which he was followed by his sons. Even Corbal smiled, whilst

Fougereot's wife slyly asked the representative if he were married himself.

"I am not. But in my case there are reasons ..." He stressed his words significantly, desiring them to understand that he was quite serious. But they laughed more heartily than ever.

"Oh, but the reasons, then?" the apple-faced woman demanded in raillery.

"The reasons?" He glared at her. "I am wedded to my duties. They leave no room for softer ties."

They began to realise that he was not jesting, and Corbal made haste to change the subject. If Chauvinière suffered him to have his way in this, it was because he required time in which to consider the impishly wicked notion that had invaded his mind.

He was still considering it when, having concluded a visit that in other times must have appeared oddly lacking in purpose, he took his way slowly down the hill to Poussignot; and he smiled a tight-lipped smile of wicked satisfaction in a notion worthy of a psychologist and humorous philosopher such as himself.

"Celibacy is an affront to Nature." That was the new gospel he was to preach, and if he knew at all the force of an idea, no matter how crack-brained, in Revolutionary France – especially an idea propounded by one in authority – there could be no doubt of its success.

The immediate sequel proved him correct. That novel mission of his he inaugurated upon the morrow. From the rostrum of the Jacobin Society of Poussignot – a society founded by a handful of hotheads, but very languidly conducted since – to the multitude assembled there by an invitation they were forced to regard as a command, he propounded his gospel with the frenzied rhetoric and specious cant with which he had learnt to sway the passions and rouse the emotions of unintelligent, unreasoning mobs.

France was being depopulated by the events. That was his exordium. The evil brood of aristocracy which the saviours of France had destroyed and were still destroying, must be replaced by a race of free men, born in an enlightened age, to make this France – this noble, emancipated France of Liberty – great and glorious among the nations of the earth. Replaced, too, must be those splendid patriots who were giving their lives so freely on the frontiers in the defence of their motherland from the invasion of the odious hirelings of despotism. To neglect this was to neglect the most sacred duty that the Nation had the right to claim from her children. It was to expose the Republic, through depopulation, to ultimate destruction.

All this tricked out in perfervid imagery, in phrases the more sonorous because hollow, gradually stirred his tatterdemalion audience to enthusiastic acclamation.

Having rendered them malleable, he hammered them now with that master-phrase of his: "Celibacy is an affront to Nature!"

Upon this theme he enlarged, expounding its moral as well as its civic and national aspects, until, at last, perceiving that he had completely taken his audience in the snare of his cant, he boldly demanded of them as a proof of patriotism and sincerity that any man who having reached the age of twenty-five remained unmarried should be declared outside the law.

Thereafter he departed in great dignity, to the acclamations of a multitude intoxicated by his verbiage.

As none knew better than Chauvinière, who made intellectual toys for himself out of these things, such was the crack-brained state of the popular mind that the more extravagant a doctrine, the more assured it was of general acceptance. Fear, moreover, now went hand in hand with imbecility. The guillotine began to function at last in Poussignot, and several recalcitrant priestly heads besides some others were shorn away. It became clear that the Citizen-Representative Chauvinière was not a man with whom it would be safe to trifle. In his wake the terror had penetrated at last to this peaceful township of the Nivernais. And in a feverish haste to give proof of patriotism there was headlong rushing into matrimony in Poussignot during the days that followed. As Chauvinière knew from his experience of mob-psychology – there was no need for him to push the matter beyond his address at the Jacobins. His crazy gospel was preached for him at street corners by unwashed orators who a month ago would not have dared to lilt their heads in Poussignot.

Within ten days the movement had reached such a pitch that it was formally proposed and unanimously agreed at the Society of Jacobins that, as the citizen-representative had propounded, for a man of twenty-five to remain unmarried in the face of the country's needs was to give proof of incivisme; to be punished as incivisme was punished by declaring him outside the law and sending him to the guillotine.

The Society of Jacobins placed its resolution in the form of an instruction before the Revolutionary Committee. But before an instruction so eccentric, the Revolutionary Committee paused in doubt, and sent for the citizen-representative to give them guidance.

'What the people will, the gods will," declared Chauvinière. "If this matter has been carried further than you would counsel or desire, yet it is not for you, the humble instruments of the People's majesty, to withstand the People's sovereign will."

His superbly oracular tone and manner overawed them. Gazing upon him and listening to him they realised that there was no God but the Goddess of Reason, and that Chauvinière was her prophet. There was no debate. And thus in the Commune of Poussignot that amazing resolution of the Jacobins was raised to the equivalent of a law. The *huissiers* of the Tribunal began upon the morrow to go forth in quest of the unmarried, to drag them before the bar, where each was given the option of finding a wife within three days, or else submitting to conviction of incivisme, with death to follow.

The intransigent were few in number, and they paid the penalty.

And now, at last, the ground was sufficiently prepared for an attack upon the hitherto unassailable *ci-devant* Vicomte de Corbal, and the gratification of the citizen-representative's monstrous sense of humour. A definite accusation of incivisme, hitherto almost impossible, was now rendered easy.

The accusation was laid, and M. Corbigny de Corbal was hailed before the bar of the Tribunal to receive the usual admonition.

To do honour to the Court and the occasion, practising that ceremony in which he believed, he had dressed himself with unusual care, in garments stored up for ceremonious occasions: a black coat with silver buttons, silk breeches and stockings and buckled shoes. His brown hair was gathered up and neatly tied in a black silk ribbon.

Very dignified and self-contained he stood in the crowded chamber of justice to hear himself admonished. When it was done he bowed gravely to the members of the Tribunal and he would have withdrawn without uttering a word, if Chauvinière had not intervened to add something of his own to the President's formal speech.

"The Citizen *ci-devant* Vicomte de Corbal," said he, in the soft accents of an advocate for the defence, "belongs by birth to a class which the Republic has abolished. Himself he has gone unscathed because of the republican spirit by which he is believed to be inspired because of the sentiments of Liberty, Equality and Fraternity by the application of which he has rendered himself esteemed. But the time is at hand when the mere appearance of republicanism may not suffice to efface the stigma of aristocratic birth, and he should perceive that he is now provided with an opportunity of placing his republicanism beyond all possibility of future question."

Chauvinière paused deliberately. An utter stillness reigned in that crowded chamber. He considered the impassive countenance of Monsieur de Corbal and anticipated with secret amusement the ruffling of that impassivity. He resumed: "Acquainted as I am with his household, in which I have had the honour to be entertained, I am fortunately in a position to advise him, to point out to him that he need not be embarrassed by any difficulties of making choice since a bride lies ready to his hand. I permit myself this indication because so often we overlook that which stands nearest, and I would not have the *ci-devant* Vicomte suffer from any such oversight. A girl of the people who is among those who serve him should prove domestically a very suitable wife. Therefore this Court counsels him not only to marry, but to marry Filomene Paulard, thus not only fulfilling the requirements of your new enactment, but also affording an abiding proof of his acceptance of the religion of equality – a religion in which France will tolerate no heretics."

The riff-raff largely composing the audience hailed the proposal uproariously as worthy of Solomon. When that uproar died down, Monsieur de Corbal at last spoke. A scarlet flush had overspread his long and rather melancholy countenance. But his voice remained calm and steady.

"You know ..." He half-turned, so as to include the entire assembly. "You all know my habits of life and of thought, and the simple creed by which I have governed my existence. I believe in communism, and I have given proofs of that belief. The Nation is above the individual, and I recognise the Nation's right to demand of me my property and, at need, my life. But I do not recognise the Nation's right to demand of me my soul—"

Chauvinière impatiently interrupted him. "We have abolished all that!"

But Corbal went on as if the interruption had not been: "Nor do I recognise the Nation's voice in this demand. With submission, citizen-judges, you were placed here to administer the existing laws and not to create new ones. The making of laws is the sole prerogative of the National Convention, and any man or group of men infringing that prerogative and arrogating to themselves any such legislative right are themselves guilty of an incivisme for which they may be indicted."

Chauvinière admired the shrewdness and subtlety of this counter-attack, and was thankful that it was made before men of too low an order of intelligence to appreciate it. A growl of anger and mockery was all it drew from the assembly, and when that subsided the President spoke without emotion: "You have three days for consideration, Citizen Corbal."

Corbal advanced a step, betrayed out of his imperturbability. The sudden perception that he stood before a wall of unreason against which intelligent argument must shatter itself in vain, drove him to momentary madness. His eyes blazed in a face that passion turned from red to white.

"Three seconds would be too much, citizen-president, for consideration; three centuries not enough to alter my resolve to reject this infamy."

And whilst the crowd surged snarling and growling, the President, impassive as doom, insisted: "Nevertheless, you have three days."

Tardily Corbal commanded himself. He reflected that further opposition now might deprive him of even those three days, which he would more than require so that he might set his house in order. He resumed his habitual dignified calm, bowed once more to the Court, and took his departure.

"You see now," said Chauvinière quietly to the President, "what it is worth, this republicanism of the *ci-devant* Vicomte. A superficial veneer underneath which we have ever the harsh, arrogant spirit of the aristocrat, a man, in his own estimation, of a different clay from that out of which the people are fashioned. He burned with shame at the thought of debasing himself in an alliance with a peasant girl. You saw that. Is that republicanism?"

And Doucier, a little sadly, bowed his head. "You are right, citizen-representative," he sighed. "It required your wit to devise a test that should reveal the man's true nature. We have been deceived in him."

Chauvinière stood up, lean and wiry, put on his plumed hat, and adjusted his cravat. "He has his choice between Filomene and the National Widow. Let us hope that he will prefer the little pullet, and that she will yet redeem him into a good republican."

Doucier laughed. He thought the citizen-representative amusing sometimes. The citizen-representative knew that he was amusing always, but that it was not given to everyone to have the wit to discern it.

Chapter Seven

At the leisurely pace of a man who meditates, M. de Corbal took his way home up the hill through the April dusk. He did not relish the thought of dying. Even less, however, did he relish the thought of the horrible *mésalliance* by which he might save his life, which shows that Chauvinière was right and that M. de Corbal's republican sentiments were not of the proper depth. The notion of supplying future Corbals with such an ancestress as Filomene was entirely repulsive to him, however much he may have esteemed Filomene in her proper place. Aristocratic sentiments, after all, die hard.

He reflected that he was confronted with a choice of evils, and he was philosopher enough to know that in such a case he must accept the less. The futility of flight was too apparent. He would be hunted down, and at a time when it was impossible to move openly in the country without papers, he would soon be overtaken and brought back in ignominy. Let him at least preserve his self-respect. Reluctant though he might be to die, life, after all, was not so delectable in these days, and the Hereafter, if the priests were right, should not be without interest.

He mounted a stile over a wall bordering one of his meadows, and as he leapt lightly down upon the turf, he was suddenly aware of a figure crouching there in the gloom. A moment he stood at gaze, then called out, challenging, whereupon the figure came upright, detached itself from the wall, and was off at speed across the narrow strip of meadowland towards the woods.

Here, thought M. de Corbal, was an eccentricity of behaviour that called for investigation. He was swift of foot, and he was upon the fugitive before the latter had covered half the distance to his goal. He clutched the shoulder of a stripling, clad in the blouse, loose pantaloons and wooden shoes of a peasant.

"A word with you, my friend. You are too fleet for honesty, to say nothing of your skulking behind a wall."

"Let me go," snarled a boyish voice. "I have done you no harm." The figure writhed in his grasp. "Don't dare to detain me!"

"Dare!" Corbal laughed. "Here's fury!"

There was more fury than the Vicomte reckoned. Something bright gleamed suddenly in the boy's hand. On the instant Corbal had him in a wrestler's grip which pinned his arms helplessly to his sides. He hugged the murderous rascal close, intending to throw him. Instead, as if contact with that young body had burnt him, he thrust it sharply from him, and stepped back.

"Name of God!" he ejaculated.

The supposed stripling stood before him, breathing hard with head a little bowed, making no further attempt to escape.

"Who are you? What are you? And why are you dressed as a man? Answer me. I will not hurt you."

The sudden gentleness of his voice, more, its high-bred inflexion, wrought a change in the other's attitude. He threw back his head, showing a face that gleamed white and ghostly in the half-light.

"Who are you? What is your name?" came the counter-questions, in a voice and delivered on a note which left Corbal little doubt of the masquerader's quality.

"Until lately I was known as the Vicomte Corbigny de Corbal. Since then I have enjoyed a certain peace as a *ci-devant*. At the moment I scarcely know how to describe myself. But this land is still mine, and that house up yonder, in which I am prepared to afford you shelter if you will deal frankly with me."

"You are a gentleman!"

"You may call me that, I hope."

"A gentleman at large in France!" Almost she seemed to laugh. "But it is a bewildering encounter."

"Mutually bewildering," said he. "I was not, myself, expecting to meet a lady."

He heard the sharp intake of her breath.

"How do you know that?"

"How? I have my intuitions. They are not to be deceived by rude garments and eccentric manners. I am at your service, madame – or, is it mademoiselle?"

She hesitated long before passionately answering him: "Oh, if you are a trickster, play your vile trick. It's all one to me. I am sick and weary. I should welcome even such rest as the guillotine brings. I am Cléonie de Montsorbier."

He repeated the name in accents of surprise.

"You are incredulous. You have heard of us in prison in Paris. We are a Nivernais family, and there should be interest in us hereabouts. You have heard, perhaps, that monsieur my father and madame my mother have already perished on the scaffold. You may even have heard that I was removed to a house of lunatics, but not that I was removed thence by a revolutionary gentleman who desired to befriend me, because possibly that is not yet known even in Paris. It's a long story, M. le Vicomte."

"Tell it me as we walk," said he, and taking her by the arm, he turned her about to face the distant house whose windows glowed ruddily in the deepening night.

As they went she told him briefly of her pseudo-secretaryship, and of her escape at La Charité from her republican protector whom she left unnamed. She had hoped to shelter at the Chateau de Blesson, with her cousins there. But to her dismay on reaching it in the dawn, she had found it closed and shuttered, the family gone. Thence on a weary horse, she had plodded on to Verrues, ten miles away, where another cousin dwelt. She found Verrues a blackened ruin, and in her exhaustion and despair, she sat down before it, and gave way to tears.

Thus she was surprised by a group of scared peasants, a half-dozen members of a family moving out to labour in the fields. She slaked all upon their being people not yet infected by revolutionary notions, and disclosed herself to them. The disclosure increased their fear. They were folk who still believed in God and the King; but who kept the belief secret lest it should bring evil days upon them.

Nevertheless it was not in their simple hearts to let a gentlewoman suffer. They gave her shelter for some days, until she began to fear the consequences to them of her being discovered there; also because to lie in hiding was too temporary a measure to suit her impatient eager spirit, she procured from them the peasant garments in which she stood, and departed, hoping to make her way on foot across the Nivernais and Burgundy, and thence slip over the frontier into Switzerland. The Nivernais she had almost crossed, for Poussignot was only a few miles distant from the confines of Burgundy. But the journey had been one of hardships beyond all that she had feared. And this notwithstanding that Fortune had singularly befriended her. She had made a practice of travelling only by night, never venturing upon roads until they were deserted. By day she would sleep hidden in some wood or buried in the straw of a barn or the hay of a stack. Twice she had been discovered, but each time by charitably disposed peasants, who, without suspecting her sex or quality, had given her food and shelter. Commonly she had suffered hunger, and once at least had been driven to steal so that she might still the pangs of it. Once she had lost her way and for two days travelled north instead of east. Nor would she have known of her error, but that in the neighbourhood of Verzy she was taken ill as the result of a drenching endured whilst endeavouring to sleep under a hedge. Here again she owed her salvation to the charity of peasants. A farm lad had found her staggering weakly along in prey to fever, and accepting the risk of yielding to his invitation she had accompanied him to his homestead, and there, since her spent condition left her no choice, she had disclosed to the mother of the household her sex and quality. For ten days she had remained there recovering health and strength, sheltered, befriended and used with every consideration. Then she had set forth once more upon her perilous journey. That was a week ago, since when her progress had been slow. She had heard of the presence in the Nivernais of the Representative Chauvinière and the consequent rousing there of revolutionary activity. Therefore she had deemed it more important to move with caution than with speed. She was upon the road by which Corbal was coming from Poussignot when she became aware of his advance. Because it was not yet quite dark, out of an excessive caution, she had slipped over the wall to avoid him, and thus had not only been discovered, but had been discovered in circumstances which naturally aroused his suspicions. It was the one error of judgment of which she had been guilty in her travels.

"Yet Fortune has again befriended you," said the Vicomte, moved at once to compassion for her suffering and admiration of her spirit. "Here at Corbal you may take a night's rest in security and comfort."

"Every such night diminishes my chances of ultimate security," he was answered on a sigh. "It is by night that I should be on my travels."

M. de Corbal halted in the porch, and surprised her by a little laugh. "Faith, mademoiselle, almost you set me an example."

"An example?"

"You suggest things ..." He broke off. "No, no. I had thought of it. It is not worthwhile." He pushed wide the door, and the glow of light from within smote them with almost blinding violence.

"Be welcome to Corbal, mademoiselle."

She stepped ahead of him into the spacious and rather shabby stone hall. He paused a moment to close and make fast the door, then turned, and his eyes, now accustomed to the light, beheld her clearly for the first time. Her grey blouse was stained and in places ragged. She had doffed the shabby hat, which looked as if it might have been filched from a scarecrow. She had cut her hair and it hung loose and ragged now about her neck and ears, just as a peasant lad's might hang, but the light smote from its golden sheen an aureole about her little head, so admirably poised, and the finely-featured high-bred face gave the lie to the tatterdemalion rest of her.

M. de Corbal gazed upon her lost in a rapture of wonder such as he had never known. So intent were these sombre dark eyes of his that at last her glance fell away before them, and she shifted a little uncomfortably.

"You were saying, monsieur?" quoth she, perhaps to break the spell. "Something of an example, was it not?"

But still he gazed and gazed, and the natural wistfulness deepened in his countenance. When at last he spoke, it was cryptically, employing the old gladiatorial formula.

"Moriturus te salutat!" He bowed a little. "Yet it is good to have seen you first."

She stared at him with closer scrutiny, startled by that well-known Latin phrase.

"What do you say? Who is it that is about to die?"

"Are we not all in that case?" he evaded, "all who are of your class and mine? Is not France to us as the arena to the Roman gladiator who hailed Caesar in those words? But I keep you standing."

The instincts of his blood asserting themselves, he remembered the duties of a host and put aside all other considerations.

"You will require garments, mademoiselle. I will call my housekeeper. Perhaps she may …"

"Ah no!" she checked him. "Clean linen if you will. Give it me yourself, or send it to me by a man if you wish. But for the rest, leave me as I am, nor disclose me to be other. The Citizen Chauvinière is a thought too close for any risks."

"You know the Citizen Chauvinière?"

She smiled. It was wonderful, he thought, that she should smile so. Not to alarm him unnecessarily she evaded his question. "I have heard of his activities."

He nodded. "You are wise, perhaps. Come then, you shall have what you need."

Himself he conducted her to a room above, procured for her the linen she required, and left her, to go and inform and instruct his household touching the presence of a peasant boy whom it pleased him to befriend.

The household, openly loyal and faithful to the Vicomte and secretly faithful to the old order, treated the visitor at table with an equality touched by deference. They had no doubt of her quality, although it is possible that her sex remained unsuspected, so slim was she and so boyish her voice. By her request the Vicomte called her Antoine, which was the name she had worn with Chauvinière.

Deep dejection sat that night upon the little company gathered there to supper in the great kitchen, and Filomene as she waited upon them showed eyes that were red from weeping in a face unusually white. They had heard the day's events before the

Revolutionary Tribunal and of the doom that now overhung their master. Filomene herself was outraged in her every sensibility by the offensive alternative to death which had been offered the Vicomte whom she served and worshipped.

Corbal alone appeared unmoved, and indifferent to the sword suspended over his head. Indeed, he was far less silent than his wont, and there was even a touch of gaiety, of exaltation in his bearing. He ministered solicitously to the needs of his guest, from whose face his eyes were removed only when she showed herself too conscious of his glance.

At first Mademoiselle de Montsorbier experienced a sense of discomfort. Those great sombre eyes riveted so ecstatically upon her evoked a memory which of all memories she desired to bury. They reminded her of another pair of eyes that smoulderingly had pondered her across another table, scorching her soul with the insult of their glance. But that sense of parallel was short-lived. The Vicomte's eyes reflected wonder and a sort of ecstasy, but all of homage. They inspired confidence, evoked a responsive kindliness, where those other eyes had awakened only fear, and somehow, before the meal was done, before the Fougereots and Filomene had retired, leaving the Vicomte and his guest alone, she had the full measure of this man. She had seen in his bearing towards his people, and their bearing towards him, his fundamental gentleness, his engaging simplicity in externals, his true nobility of heart and the devotion he was capable of inspiring. The pale, handsome face under its neatly dressed lustrous brown hair was the face of a loyal, generous man, in whom no woman need hesitate to repose her trust.

He took no advantage of the circumstances to seek to detain her there alone in talk. Himself, soon after the departure ol the others, he escorted her to the chamber set apart for her. He set down her candle, requested her commands, and withdrew after wishing her a good rest with an austerity which left nothing to be desired, and without so much as an attempt to kiss her fingertips, which in all the circumstances would have been no more than proper.

Chapter Eight

"Mademoiselle, remain yet another day with us. The more complete now your rest, the better speed will you make hereafter, so that the time will not be lost."

Thus M. de Corbal to his guest on the following afternoon.

They sat in the library, whither he had earlier conducted her; an untidy, dusty room, panelled in soiled white on all sides but one, which was packed from floor to ceiling with serried ranks of books. Its furnishings were handsome and as massive as anything produced in the reign of Louis XV, but they wore, like all else in that house, an air of dilapidation. The litter on the spacious writing-table testified at once to studious industry and to negligence.

Mademoiselle de Montsorbier, occupying a window-seat along which was stretched one of her slim, pantalooned legs, demurred at the proposal, expressed the opinion that she had best push on at dusk; that, in fact, she could not think of subjecting M. le Vicomte to the risk of her discovery under his roof.

At this M. de Corbal laughed with such evident amusement as to pique her a little, for she could not conceive in what she was ridiculous. But he did not leave her long in conjecture. He paced the chamber as he talked, upright and handsome, looking more like a nobleman and less like other things than usual. Not only had he resumed today the ceremonious dress in which yesterday he had attended the Tribunal – the only suit of its kind in his wardrobe – but he had improved upon it. There was a foam of lace at his neck, and ruffles at his wrists to veil the hands which labour in the open had burnt brown, and he had brought out of their neglect a pair of lacquered shoes with paste buckles and red heels, shoes which in those days would have imperilled any mans neck.

He explained his laughter. "Mademoiselle, I am in the enviable position of a man for whom risks have ceased to exist, whom fear can no longer touch. This is Tuesday, and on Thursday next I am to die. That is why I laugh at the notion of danger to me from harbouring you."

She swung her leg from the window-seat, and sat bolt upright, confronting him, her eyes wide.

"Monsieur! How is this possible? You amuse yourself at my expense! How can it be that you, who are free …"

"I will explain," he interrupted her, and he did so.

She heard his tale in growing distress and also in growing admiration for his intrepid calm, for the almost humorous outlook with which he viewed his desperate situation. Again she was reminded of another whose outlook was ever humorous, too. But the difference!

"The beast!" she said, when he had done. "The cruel, mocking beast!"

The Vicomte nodded. "That describes him, I think. He is facetiously malign. Well, well! He may have my head. But he will not make me bow it to his humorous will."

Her hands twisting and untwisting between her knees in her agitation of concern, she began to urge him to seek safety in flight.

He cut her short at the very outset.

"I thought of it, of course. But it would be useless, and there's a degradation in failure to which I will not expose myself. I'll be no quarry for these revolutionary dogs to hunt. If succumb I must, I'll succumb in dignity, as my blood demands. You agree, I hope, that the alternative is unthinkable; that every dead Corbal would shudder in his grave if I were guilty of any baseness to save my useless life?"

She pondered him in silence with an infinite compassion, an infinite tenderness. She was little addicted normally to seek the feminine relief of tears. Yet now, it was only by an effort of will that she repressed them.

"Is there," she asked after a moment, "no third course possible? Have you thought well, monsieur?"

Perhaps more of her tender concern escaped in her voice than she intended. He halted before her, and his dark solemn eyes considered her. The pallor deepened in his face as if he were suddenly beset by fear, and a deeper wistfulness crept into the lines of it. At last, very slowly, he answered her.

"Yes, I have thought. And a third course does offer. But …" He broke off with a little gesture of despair.

"But what, monsieur? Express it freely. It is the way to test a thought."

"You know that, too! How wise you are!" Admiration flashed in his eyes. "This thing, however, is not in need of the test of expression. I hesitate only from the fear of being misunderstood."

She almost smiled as she looked up at him. "To a man in your case can it matter to be misunderstood? And misunderstood by whom? By me? For what does my opinion count in this?"

"For everything," he answered, and set her staring and a little breathless, stirred by something quite indefinable.

He swung away from her abruptly, paced to the book-lined wall, and back again, with bowed head, to come to a halt once more before her.

"I may be suspected of having found here no more than something to supply my need. That is my great fear. Will you believe me, mademoiselle, if I swear that I shall utter no word that is not true? I am a man in his last hours. There may be little good in me; but never in life have I soiled myself by falsehood."

"That is how I should judge you, monsieur. Speak freely, then."

He spoke, but not freely. He faltered and stumbled awkwardly in a manner utterly unusual to him, whose utterance normally was precise and scholarly.

"You will not see, mademoiselle, I beseech you, a lack of—of homage in what I am to say. In other circumstances … But here time presses. I am a man who has lived much alone. My books and my land have been my only concerns, and my little family almost my only company in years. It is this aloofness from the world which has made possible my survival until now. Many things that make up the life of my kind have passed me by. I have not missed them, because I have not desired them. No woman … I beg you to believe me … No woman has ever touched my life. Until now."

Mademoiselle de Montsorbier stiffened. She was very white, and the grey woollen smock shuddered under the heave of her slight breasts. The Vicomte paused there, watching her almost in fear, he who had contemplated death with such tranquillity. He clasped his hands in his nervousness and found them moist.

"I—I have read the poets, of course. Yet I do not know how these things come to a man. I know only that love has come to me like a lightning stroke out of heaven. Bear with me, mademoiselle, though I may seem to you outrageous. Doubt what you will, but not my truth and sincerity."

Again he paused. But still she said nothing. Of the two it would have been hard to say which was possessed by the deeper fear.

"When first I saw you there in the light last night, it seemed to me … as if my soul leapt from me to embrace your soul. I utter crudities, perhaps. I can express it in no other way. But so spontaneous, so—so inevitable was this thing, that it has seemed to me … It is not a presumption, mademoiselle. It is an instinct, I think. It has seemed to me that something reciprocal, something mutual must have taken place. It seemed impossible that a man's spirit could … experience so much … unsupported.

"Mademoiselle, I am ashamed of my poor words. They do not—"

She interrupted him at last. She had risen, and, unbelievable miracle as it seemed to him, her breast was leaning on his own, her face, all white and piteous, was upturned to him.

"Ashamed!" she cried. "Ashamed!" There was a music of tenderness in her voice that dazed his senses. "Your words leave nothing unsaid. Nothing that is not true, at least. Your instincts were at no fault, my dear."

His arms went round her. His voice was the voice of a man in pain.

"Love is the fulfilment of every living thing, and I might have died unfulfilled if you had not come to me at the eleventh hour."

She shuddered. "Oh, my dear!" She lay faint against him.

"Ah! But all that is changed," he cried, to hearten her. "You make life possible. If I had been mistaken, if you had not cared, nothing further would have mattered. I should still have died the richer, the nobler for what you brought me. But since you care ... Listen, my dear. The decree of the Revolutionary Tribunal is only that I marry. So that I marry within three days I fulfil the requirement of this grotesque mockery which they call a law. Filomene was proposed to me, because I would make no choice for myself. But Filomene or another, it is all one to them. If you, then, come with me before the Tribunal in peasant dress – that will be safer – as a girl whom I prefer, whom I have chosen for myself ... We can invent your place of origin. That will not be difficult. If, then ..."

She broke away from him, and stepped back. "Oh, you don't know what you are saying!" she cried out in deep distress.

He stood crestfallen, his soaring hopes all checked.

"But if—if ... we love each other?" he faltered. "What difficulty, then? Need the notion of an immediate marriage be so repugnant?"

"It isn't that. It isn't that."

"What then?"

She laughed without mirth. The situation, after all, was not without mirthless humour. "Chauvinière!" she said significantly.

"Chauvinière?" he echoed, misunderstanding her of course. "What of him, then? Even Chauvinière will be silenced since his demand that I marry will be satisfied. He named Filomene as the only bride at hand. But one woman will do as well as another for him; or if not for him, at least for the Tribunal. So that I obey the decree they can hardly compel me in the matter of my choice. That were too dangerous a precedent."

"What you say would be true in the case of any woman but myself."

"But yourself?" He gazed bewildered.

"Because I am the one woman of whom Chauvinière will not permit you to make choice. It is sadly, cruelly ironical, my friend. If you disclose me you merely destroy me with yourself."

"If I disclose you as Mademoiselle de Montsorbier. But that is not the intention. As a peasant, a girl of the people—"

She interrupted him, to make all plain at last.

"That might serve for the others. But not for Chauvinière. Chauvinière was the deputy who smuggled me out of Paris."

It was a long moment before he completely understood, and understanding brought a curious horror. "It was he? It was he …"

She nodded, her little features twisted in a bitter smile.

He shuddered, and put his hands to his face to shut out the picture which the sight of her now evoked. He stepped back, and sat down abruptly in a chair. He groaned as he sat there, and at first she misunderstood the source of his pain, imagined it to lie only in the sudden sense of defeat which her disclosure brought him. But his words enlightened her.

"Chauvinière!" he muttered. "That ineffable beast! His foul eyes crawling over your purity and grace." He set his teeth. "That he should have dared! That he should have soiled you by his glance!"

"My dear, is it worthwhile to think of that? At such a moment?"

"What else is there to think of? What else can matter by comparison? My life!" he laughed. "I would give it freely to have spared you!"

There was a tap at the door. Filomene came in with a scared countenance. "It is the citizen-representative," she announced. "He is here. He asks to see you."

Mademoiselle de Montsorbier shrank back in fear.

Corbal uncovered his face, and came slowly to his feet.

"The citizen-representative?" he questioned dully. "Chauvinière?" Then, abruptly, he cast off his dejection. He squared his shoulders and stood stiff and straight, his face alight with purpose. Mademoiselle de Montsorbier, observing him, instead of distress beheld in him only a preternatural calm. And when presently he spoke again, not only had his voice resumed its natural level tone, but it was faintly changed with a note that was almost derisive.

"The Citizen-Representative Chauvinière, eh? Is he alone?"

"Yes, monsieur. I saw no one else."

The Vicomte nodded. He was smiling. "But how very good, how very condescending of the citizen-representative to honour my house again! And so very opportunely! Almost it is as if he had guessed my need to see him, and desired to spare me the trouble of going in quest of him. Let him wait a moment or two in the hall, Filomene. Detain him there if you can. Then bring him in."

Between surprise and relief at the Vicomte's manner, Filomene departed.

Before she was out of the room, Corbal was at a tall cupboard of polished mulberry that stood against the wall. He found Mademoiselle de Montsorbier at his elbow.

"Will you hide me in there?"

He lost a second in staring at her. Then he smiled and shook his head. "I have no thought to hide you." He took a mahogany case from a shelf in the cupboard.

"But if he finds me here!"

"It is what I desire." He took up a powder horn and a little linen bag, and closed the door of the cupboard. "The confident, overbearing fool!"

He crossed to his writing-table, and opened the box. It contained a brace of duelling pistols, bedded in its red velvet lining.

Chapter Nine

Filomene had her attractions, and a man of so enterprising a nature as the citizen-representative does not allow feminine attractions to go unheeded.

When she returned to him where he waited in the hall, he took her softly rounded chin in his lean hand and considered her approvingly. His words, however, suggested that he did so dispassionately, in a spirit of critical detachment.

"Does he perceive your graces yet, my dear, this fastidious *ci-devant?* Faith, in his place, I should not wait to be bidden twice. I'll make a *ci-devant* Vicomtesse of you yet," he promised, and kissed her by way of sealing the bargain. Detachment, after all, may be pushed too far, and he had a way with him, the Citizen-Representative Chauvinière.

He released her chin and bade her conduct him to the reluctant bridegroom. But Filomene remembered her orders to detain him, and he, himself, had afforded her the pretext. More than this, it was suddenly revealed to her how she might even save the Vicomte for whom her affection was of the exalted kind that desires to express itself only in service.

"It's not only the bridegroom who is reluctant," said she, her winsome face grown sullen. "You make very free with a poor girl, you gentlemen of the Revolutionary Tribunal. You bid a man marry me without so much as a 'by-your-leave' to me. You take it for granted that I've no mind in the matter. 'Marry Filomene on Thursday, or we guillotine you on Friday.'" She sniffed her angry scorn. "You think that's all there is to it. And what if Filomene doesn't want the man you order to become her husband?"

Chauvinière was scowling at her. He remembered the soft glances he had seen her bestow upon Corbal, which had first suggested to him the course he had taken. His scowl became a smile of mockery.

"What game do you play with me, my girl?"

"No game, citizen-representative. It's deadly earnest as you and your Tribunal will discover. I'm not to be handed over like a cow or a sheep, and I don't belong to you to be bestowed by you. Liberty, eh? That's your notion of liberty, is it? Why, the aristocrats would never have dared so much, and you'll not dare it where I am concerned."

"But of course not, if you say so."

"I do say so." Her voice grew shrill. She had wrought herself into a fine mimic passion. "You'd better understand me clearly, and save yourselves the trouble of pushing this imbecile business any further. I do not take a husband at your bidding, and certainly not the Citizen Corbal. I refuse to marry."

Chauvinière was smiling tolerantly upon the vehemence.

"You do?" quoth he.

"Flatly," she announced, not without a flash of exultation, conceiving that thus she had checkmated Chauvinière and saved her beloved Vicomte from the peril that assailed him.

Chauvinière, still smiling, fetched a sigh. "A pity!" he said. "A thousand pities! He will now, if he wishes to live, have to find someone for himself, and I cannot hope that he will find anyone half so agreeable." He sighed again, inwardly relishing the joke. "Now lead me to him, if you please."

Filomene shrank back, aghast to find her weapons so easily shivered. She choked down her tears of rage, eyeing the citizen-representative with a malevolence that but increased his secret mirth.

Then, nothing else being left to do, she conducted him in silence and announced him to the waiting Vicomte. Lithe and active in his long grey coat, tricolour sash, from which a sabre now dangled and cockaded plumed hat which he did not trouble to remove,

Chauvinière swaggered into the library. Within the threshold he halted, irony in every line of him, to survey the Vicomte who, with hands behind him, stood placidly by the empty fireplace. He jerked a thumb after the retreating Filomene.

"A juicy pullet, my friend; not to be boggled over by a man of taste."

"Perhaps I am not a man of taste – by revolutionary canons."

"In your own interests I hope you'll prove so. You've offended the child by your reluctance, and she declares that you shall not marry her now if you would. But that's to be overcome by a little persuasive wooing. In your place, I should offer it. You'll find her arms warmer about your neck than the collar of the guillotine. But it's for you to choose between maid and widow."

"You repeat yourself, citizen. Is that the only purpose of your visit?"

Chauvinière's light eyes drew narrow. Here was one who dealt in a mockery that was deadlier than his own, and just as elusive.

"You misapprehend me." His tone was dry and crisp. "It is the fault of your class to want for understanding. It is the emptiness of aristocrat heads that has brought so many of them to the basket. I am here, my dear *ci-devant,* to exhort you in the fraternal spirit …"

He broke off. A slight movement in the corner on his right drew his glance aside, to discover there a slim lad in peasant blouse and pantaloons.

"Why? Who's this that …" Again he checked, a sudden quickening in his glance. He leaned forward, staring hard; took a short step, and slopped again. Then an oath of amazement escaped him, and on the heels of that a laugh, loud and lull of relish. "Why, here's a meeting!" He swept off his hat. "It becomes necessary to uncover." He bowed. "And how long may you have been at Corbal, my dear secretary?"

Mademoiselle de Montsorbier came forward a little, miraculously preserving her composure.

"Since last night, citizen," she answered simply, so simply and calmly that it staggered him.

"Oh, since last night, citizen!" he mimicked her. "Since last night, eh? Name of a name! I find more at Corbal than I should have dreamed of seeking. Life is full of surprises. But they are seldom as pleasant." He moved to advance towards her.

"Stand where you are!"

It was Corbal who spoke, in a cold, crisp tone that effectively arrested the representative. He stiffened as he confronted the Vicomte across half the room.

"Life is full of surprises, as you say, citizen-representative. This one may not prove quite as pleasant as you are supposing."

There was in the Vicomte's attitude, in his very calm, something sinister and menacing.

Instantly Chauvinière scented danger, and as instantly would he have forestalled it; but he was hampered and undone by the mockery in which he dealt so lavishly. His absurd gesture of mock-deference, cumbered now his right hand with his doffed hat. Before he could slip that hand into his bosom to pluck thence the pistol which he carried ready for just such emergencies, it was necessary to be rid of the hat. He tucked it swiftly under his left arm. But he got no farther.

His movement was the danger signal to Corbal, and Corbal now covered him with a heavy duelling pistol, steadied upon his left forearm.

"Move a finger, citizen-representative, and I'll dispatch you into Hell."

Chauvinière obeyed, but none too literally. He planted his feet wide, and folded his hands behind him. Then he laughed. He seemed entirely unperturbed, dissembling by an easy bearing the watchfulness of those light eyes of his.

"Surprise upon surprise!" said he. "And this from you, my dear *ci-devant*. I was far, indeed, from expecting it of you. Hitherto you have been of so charming and unfailing a courtesy that I should never have thought you capable of such a grossness. Why should you desire to intimidate me?"

"You misapprehend me. I am not proposing to intimidate you."

"What then?"

"To kill you."

Again Chauvinière laughed, although he paled a little under his tan.

"But what words! Come, citizen; let us be practical. How can my death serve you? Will it, do you suppose, save you from the obligation of complying with the decree of the Revolutionary Tribunal, or, in the alternative, of leaving your head on the guillotine? A little reflection, my friend, will show you that it will merely precipitate your doom."

The Vicomte remained unperturbed. "And a little reflection on your side will show you that my life being already forfeit, I can lose nothing by killing you."

"But an act of such puerile and fruitless vindictiveness!" Chauvinière seemed shocked and hurt. "Besides, my friend, I have two men with me, out there. If you imagine that to shoot me will afford you a chance of escape, you are wrong. The sound of the shot will bring in my men, and that will be the end of you."

"If that were true, which I know it not to be, the intervention would still come too late to prevent the end of you. And Mademoiselle de Montsorbier, at least, will have been made safe. Also you will have expiated the unforgivable presumption which led you to raise your rascal's eyes to her. You son of a dog! You gutter-begotten rogue! Your very glance has been a defilement to her. A slug crawling over the white purity of a lily's petal."

"We become lyrical!" said Chauvinière, but there was a snarl in his voice, for inwardly his arrogant soul was writhing under the lash of the nobleman's contemptuous insults. "I understand, I think. Well, well, you have me at a disadvantage. I must make terms, I suppose."

"There are no terms to be made. It but remains that you give the only payment you can afford."

"You mean that you intend to murder me in cold blood! It is inconceivable. After all, you are a gentleman, not an assassin." There was no mockery now in Chauvinière's voice. It was warmly earnest. "At least, let us exchange shots, here in this room – at ten paces, or any distance that you please elsewhere. You cannot do less than that."

Monsieur de Corbal resumed his urbanity. "I am desolated to refuse you even that. If it were a question only of myself, of my own life and liberty, I would accede gladly. Indeed, I doubt if I should be at even so much trouble to preserve them. But there is Mademoiselle de Montsorbier. I cannot allow either her fate or the punishment of the insult your attentions have put upon her to lie at the mercy of luck or markmanship."

Chauvinière's face had turned grey. "I am to be murdered, then?"

"Not murdered. Executed."

"A fine distinction!"

"You have dealt a little freely yourself in fine distinctions where the anguish of others was concerned. It is just that a man should sometimes drink as he has poured." The Vicomte's cold sternness left little doubt of the measure of his resolve. Without moving his eyes from Chauvinière, he spoke to Mademoiselle de Montsorbier.

"Mademoiselle, may I beg you to withdraw?"

"My God!" broke in a groan from the representative's bloodless lips, his arrogant spirit now subdued entirely. Only the Vicomte's fixed stare and the conviction that his least movement must hasten the approaching doom prevented him from taking the chance of reaching for that pistol in his bosom. Though fear might have him now in an icy grip, yet his wits retained their clarity. To the last second he would wait and watch for his opportunity. Therefore was he still careful to do nothing to precipitate an end that might yet be averted.

"If you please, mademoiselle!" The Vicomte repeated almost peremptorily, for mademoiselle had made no movement to obey him.

She moved at last, but not to depart.

"A moment please," she said. She strove with her agitation. "Let us be practical, as the citizen-representative himself began by suggesting."

Touched though she might be by the terrible intransigent demands of the Vicomte's devotion, she realised the futility of sacrificing a chance of escape and safety, which she dimly perceived, to the exploitation of a romantic vindictiveness. She saw more clearly and farther than the Vicomte. She had less resentment to blind her. To be desired by a man, however unworthy, can never be quite so unpardonable an offence in the eyes of a woman as in those of her accepted lover. Therefore her thirst for Chauvinière's blood was less fierce than the Vicomte's. It might go unslaked so that his life should serve them better than his death.

Calmly now she expounded her proposals.

"The citizen-representative spoke just now of making terms. Let him write three lines, informing the Revolutionary Tribunal of Poussignot that he has found it necessary suddenly to pay a visit to Nevers, which will keep him absent until tomorrow. After that, let him consent to be confined here for twenty-four hours, so as to give us that measure of start in our escape. Those are the terms on which you will no doubt, agree, Vicomte, to spare his life."

The Vicomte's face darkened. "I should prefer—"

She interrupted him, her tone persuasively insistent. "I have told you, my friend, what I desire. It is, believe me, better, safer so; nor do I want you to soil your hands unnecessarily."

It he yielded grudgingly, at least he wasted no words.

"It is for you to command. Be it so. You have heard mademoiselle's proposal, citizen, What do you say?"

Chauvinière breathed more freely. The tide of his courage flowed again, bringing with it at once a resumption of his normal manner. If he accepted this chance of life, he certainly should not be suspected of snatching at it.

He took now his time in answering, let it be seen that he pondered the proposal in dignified calm.

"As I have already said, you have me at a disadvantage." He shrugged. "I must therefore capitulate on the terms you offer. But I'll first require some guarantee that when I have fulfilled my part, you will not fail to perform yours."

"My word is your guarantee," said Corbal, curtly.

Chauvinière pursed his lips. "A little meagre," he deprecated.

"It has never yet been so accounted. And only a fellow of your own base origin, ignorant of the ways of men of honour, could suppose it."

Chauvinière looked at him, and sneered. "It is evidently among the ways of men of honour to insult the man at whose head they hold a pistol. That is noble. That inspires confidence. That assures one that the word of such a man is a sufficient guarantee of anything!" He was bitterly derisive. "But I must take my chance of your keeping faith. I see that plainly. Tell me this at least: when you have departed, and the twenty-four hours shall have come to an end, who is to restore me to liberty?"

"I shall arrange for that."

"You'll forgive my importunity in desiring to know something of those arrangements before I surrender completely to your wishes. You'll realise my reluctance to be left to starve in the cellar into which you'll lock me if you should forget, or find it difficult, to take the necessary steps to procure my release."

It was mademoiselle who answered him. "At this hour tomorrow the key of your prison shall be delivered to the President of the Revolutionary Committee together with a note containing the information necessary to procure your enlargement."

He inclined his head. "That will do excellently, of course. But who will carry the key and the note?"

"You may depend upon us to find a messenger, wherever we may be. There is no difficulty in that."

"But messengers are sometimes unreliable. If this one should delay or neglect entirely to discharge his errand?"

"We shall do our best to procure a messenger entirely trustworthy, and we shall assure him of a handsome reward at your hands to quicken his zeal. That is the utmost we can do. The rest is your risk."

He shrugged and spread his hands. "I must accept it, I suppose. You leave me little choice."

"About it, then," Corbal commanded him. "Write your note here. You will find quills, ink and paper."

Chauvinière stepped forward as he was bidden, drew up a chair and sat down at the writing-table, across which the Vicomte laced him with his ever-levelled pistol.

His pen scratched industriously for some moments, but not half so industriously as his nimble rascally wits, seeking for him a way out of this trap, a way of breaking faith and turning the tables on these two who made a mock of him.

At last he signed with a flourish, flung down the pen and rose. He took up the note and thrust it under the eyes of Monsieur de Corbal at close quarters; at such close quarters that his left hand which held it was not more than three inches from the Vicomte's right with its levelled pistol.

"Read for yourself," he said harshly.

Momentarily Monsieur de Corbal's glance was lowered to read. But in that moment the sheet waved and fell away under his eyes; and before he realised what was happening, the fingers of the hand which had held it had pounced upon his wrist and their paralysing grip was bending it aside so that the Vicomte's weapon was now harmlessly deflected.

Corbal saw the representatives right hand slide into the bosom of his broad-lapelled coat for the pistol which he kept there, and heard the representative's mocking voice.

"I take this trick, I think, my dear *ci-devant*. Opportunity never fails the man who knows how to seize it."

And his laughter rang out clear and sharp to be suddenly lost in the report of a shot which filled the room with its reverberations.

Chauvinière choked on his laugh, loosed his hold of the Vicomte's wrist and reeled backwards, whilst the pistol which he had been in the act of drawing dropped from his nerveless grasp. He brought up with his shoulders to the wall, pressing to his left side a hand which grew red almost at once with the blood oozing between the fingers.

Steadying himself there, his features twisted into a spasmodic grin. He attempted to speak, but broke into a cough, with the acrid taste of powder-smoke in his throat and nostrils. The cough deepened. It became a frantic effort to clear his lungs so that he might breathe, and a foam of blood appeared upon his lips. He writhed yet an instant, his limbs twitched convulsively, and finally he slid down the panelled wall into a quiet heap from which his knees protruded sharply.

It had all happened so quickly that the Vicomte had never moved from his place beyond the table, nor mademoiselle from the other end of the room, where she stood staring white-faced upon her work, the pistol still smoking in her hand.

It is curious that the first thing calling for comment from Monsieur de Corbal should have been the least important.

"Death caught him with laughter on his lips," he said on a note of horror.

"I seem to remember," said mademoiselle, "that once he predicted something of the kind for himself." Her voice was oddly strained.

The Vicomte pursued his train of thought.

"He might be laughing still, and with good reason, if you had not insisted upon taking the second pistol for your own possible emergencies. I never dreamed that the emergency would be mine. You were only just in time, Cléonie. Already I was looking in the face of death."

"That," she answered unsteadily, "was my only justification." She shuddered, let her pistol fall to the ground at last, covered her face with her hands and fell to sobbing convulsively.

Instantly the Vicomte was at her side, his arms round her slim shoulders, his head bending to hers, his voice soothing and heartening her. Thus he drew her from the room, closing the door upon the thing it contained, and out into the hall, where Filomene with a scared face awaited them.

Chapter Ten

Seated out there in the chill gloom of the hall, on a high-backed wooden settle ranged against the grey wall, Mademoiselle de Montsorbier presently recovered command of herself.

She looked from Filomene, who, without illusions now on the score of this visitor's sex, knelt at her feet, chafing one of her hands, to M. de Corbal, who leaned over her in a solicitude that made him momentarily oblivious of all else.

"My friend, forgive this weakness, it is not the time to yield to it. Tears are a luxury for those who are secure." She dried her eyes. "We are in grave peril now, and it will need all our resource to win out of it."

But M. de Corbal smiled confidently. "Your resource has already provided for that, my dear. The note which you made him write to the members of the Tribunal will sufficiently explain his absence, whilst his removal raises the only obstacle to—to the nuptials which are required of me, provided that—that you—"

She interrupted him, raising her eyes to his, a wan smile on her white face. "You may take that for granted now, Raoul."

"Then let us lose no time. Filomene will find you such garments as you need, and we'll present ourselves to the Tribunal at once. Its members are all friendly towards me in themselves. It was only Chauvinière's influence and the fear of him which stiffened them against me in the matter of these revolutionary nuptials. In Chauvinière's absence they'll be willing enough to let me choose my own bride so that I comply with the decree. Indeed, not Chauvinière himself could have pushed matters so far as to constrain my choice of a wife, so long as I was willing to take one, especially if she were of humble origin as you'll pretend to be. Come, then. We'll invent the origin, together with a name for you, as we go."

"How you run on," she said, and almost laughed for all her heart-sickness and abiding horror of the thing so lately done.

"It is necessary. Time presses. Come."

"Wait! Wait!" she was imperative. "Do not let haste drive us into rashness. Consider first what must follow. Chauvinière's note will satisfy the Tribunal now, no doubt. But for how long? In a day or two there will be questions ..."

He broke in upon her fears. "You do not know Poussignot. I do. I have lived here all my days. Trust my judgment in this. Chauvinière's presence has been a nightmare upon the place. His absence will bring relief, a reaction to the normal which will steadily grow whilst that absence is protracted. Very soon Poussignot's only concern will be lest Chauvinière should return. Poussignot will do nothing to encourage that, and will rest content so long as it does not occur."

"You are very confident."

"I have cause to be."

He was persuading her. "And the note?" she asked. "How will you convey it to the Tribunal?"

"Oh, I've thought of that, too. The ostler at the inn where Chauvinière lodges is my man Fougereot's nephew, a God-fearing lad to whom all *sansculottes* are detestable. Fougereot will convey the note to him, and he will deliver it: a natural enough messenger."

Her face brightened at last. "You've thought of everything," she approved him. "Chauvinière's death, then—"

"Is the best thing that could have happened for the world in general and ourselves in particular. And he brought it on himself, overreaching himself in his trickiness. Fetch Fougereot from the fields, Filomene. Meanwhile I'll get the note."

The girl departed on her errand, and the Vicomte returned to the library. Alone with her thoughts, Mademoiselle de Montsorbier fell momentarily to shuddering again, and again covered her face with her hands to shut out the sight of Chauvinière as she had last seen him. Thus M. de Corbal found her on his return. She heard him close the door of the library and turn the key in the lock. Then seeing her huddled there, he hastened to her side. "My dear, my dear! Courage! Courage!"

"I need it, yes." Her pale lips were twisted into a smile, half-grim, half-whimsical. "I am not used to killing men."

"If I could have spared you that!" he cried. "But you have no grounds for self-reproach." And he reasoned with her long to banish from her mind the horror by which he perceived her to be beset. At last his fond efforts prevailed.

"Yes, yes. You are right. This is sheer weakness. And it's out of season. You have the note?" He held it up in silence. "Read it to me. Let us know exactly what he has written."

The daylight was beginning to fade. He strode across to the mullioned window, and with his shoulder turned towards her raised the sheet so as to hold it to the light. In that attitude he remained for a long while immovable and silent, until at last her patience ended.

"Well!" she urged him. "Read it to me."

He turned to her still in silence, and she saw that his face was of the colour of chalk.

"What is it!" she cried in immediate alarm.

He uttered a little laugh of bitterness, of hopelessness.

"I seem to remember that the rascal said the trick was his. A trick, indeed. Come here." She crossed to his side at once. "See for yourself what he has written, the bitter jester."

She took the sheet from his hand, and read: "My dear *ci-devant* – this is to assure you that within the next twenty-four hours two things of interest to you will happen: you will be guillotined and the dainty, slippery Montsorbier will at last belong to me. I shall have cause to thank you for the entertainment provided for me here today."

She looked up at M. de Corbal in blank dismay. The Vicomte nodded, smiling bitterly. "He counted confidently upon tricking me with it as he did, the resourceful dog; so confidently that he didn't hesitate to indulge his wicked humour even with my pistol at his head."

"Yes," she said. "He was like that. And his humour was the death of him."

They looked at each other helplessly, almost despairingly, bereft of the staff upon which they had so confidently looked to lean.

They were back, it seemed, in the situation which had been theirs that afternoon before the advent of Chauvinière, save that now they were additionally burdened with the representative's dead body. There could no longer be any question of those revolutionary nuptials upon which they had been counting. For in the absence of any acceptable explanation for it, Chauvinière's disappearance must very soon give rise to inquiry. At any moment almost that inquiry might begin. Even if he had not announced to any his intention of visiting Corbal, some there might have been who had seen him come that way. He was not a man whose movements went unnoticed. He could not pass anywhere unperceived. The trail, even if weak in places, would presently lead to the Chateau de Corbal. The Vicomte would be asked questions which he could not answer. To hide the body could not avail him. He would be required to produce the living Chauvinière. And failing that, the conclusion was foregone. It needed no words between them to expound all this. Each saw it clearly.

"There is one thing only, now," said the Vicomte. "I must go. I must set out at once before the hunt is up."

She looked at him, her bright face resolute. "We must go, you mean."

He shook his head. "Do you think I'll link you to a hunted man?"

"You will be hunted for the thing I did."

"What then? The thing you did was done to save me. It was made necessary by my own carelessness. The responsibility for the deed is mine. The intention to kill him in any case was mine. Only an accident, my own stupidity, prevented it."

"All that is not worth discussion," said she. "There are more important things to consider." And that she was considering them her knit brows bore witness.

"Yes, yes," he agreed. "You must shift for yourself now, my dear. It would not be wise in you to remain. I'll try to think of something for you. All that I can think at the moment – though it breaks my heart to say it – is that in no case must you come with me."

Again she looked at him, and now she was faintly, sadly smiling.

"How far do you think that you will get in your flight through this mad land?"

"That's why; that's why," he answered passionately. "I know I stand hardly a chance at all."

"Without me you stand none. That is why you need me more than ever. We are to be married. That was agreed between us. Shall I let a husband slip through my fingers without an effort?"

"Can you jest, Cléonie?" His voice was shaken with pain.

"Ah, but I can be serious, too," she said, now oddly tender. She set her hands upon his shoulders and looked up into his pale, distressed countenance. "Do you believe in Destiny, my dear?"

"I don't know what I believe."

"Consider then. Do you think it is just blind chance that you and I, who without knowing it have been seeking each other from the beginning of our lives, should have been brought together in this odd manner, at this odd time, in circumstances which left us no leisure for ordinary wooing? My dear, don't you see that it is Destiny which has linked us now? If I had not come when I came, you would certainly have perished. If I had not found you when I did, it is probable that I should have perished too. Perceiving this, can you suppose that our lives are to end here, now that we have met?"

Her earnestness shook him, and partly he succumbed, as men will – especially men in desperate case – to the suggestion that behind all human fortunes there is a guiding intelligence which may not be thwarted. Nevertheless, for her sake, because of the risk he perceived for her, he still resisted, though more weakly now, her intention to join him in his flight.

"But if we separate," she said with sad conviction, "we separate for ever; there is no chance for either of us. I feel it. I know it. Together we may win out. If we do not, at least we shall be together to the end, as Destiny intends for us. And it is my strong belief that we are meant for a happier union than the crazy republican nuptials with which you would have been content."

He looked at her in heavy silence, looked down into those clear, steady, fearless eyes, and surrendered at last to her dauntless spirit. He drew her close and kissed her gently.

"So be it, my dear. I leave myself to you; to you and Destiny."

She flashed him a quick smile, and at once became brisk and practical. She demanded to be made free of his wardrobe that she might find herself male garments better suited to the part she meant to play. Naturally he desired to know what part this was, what plan was in her mind.

Lightly she mocked him. "You thought of course that I should be a party to a blind, blundering flight that would land us headlong in destruction. But I am proposing an orderly retreat. I have it here." She tapped her golden head. "The details are yet to be thought out. That while I change my clothes. Ask me no questions now, my friend. Trust me and leave yourself to me, as you said just now you would do."

It was generous of him to thrust aside a momentary vexation at this half-confidence. "Have your way, then, Madame Destiny," he said, "I have made unconditional surrender."

Chapter Eleven

Having placed at her disposal the slender resources of his wardrobe, M. de Corbal left her, and went to make his own preparations for immediate departure. He gathered up what store of money he possessed, a little secret hoard of gold which he disposed in a hollow belt next to his skin, and a bundle of assignats, to be spent on their way to the frontier, since they would be useless beyond, should they ever cross it. There were, too, a few family jewels which – since sentiment must yield to necessity – might later, abroad, be converted into money, and lastly some title-deeds and other papers establishing possessions very insecure at present but to become valuable again should France ever awaken from her republican nightmare. Since to take all was out of the question, it became necessary to select the most important, and this selection occupied some little time.

Almost an hour had elapsed before he descended to the hall, booted and spurred, carrying cloak and valise, for she had told him that they would ride openly as soon as darkness should have fallen. It had fallen now and it was in the light of a cluster of candles that he found her already awaiting him, arrayed in garments which, despite their ridiculous looseness, gave her something of the *petit-maître* air which she had worn as Chauvinière's secretary. Considering the amazing things that she had done with scissors and needle, her speed in making ready seemed nothing short of miraculous. And there were signs that her preparations had been completed some time ago, and that she had since been engaged with arrangements which really should have been his care. For even as M. de Corbal was descending the stairs, he heard her addressing Fougereot who at that moment came in from the open.

Her voice rang sharply. "You are just in time, Fougereot. Here is M. le Vicomte. Have you made everything ready?"

"Everything as mademoiselle commanded," the man replied, and so informed M. de Corbal not only that she had disclosed her identity to his people, but also that she had been issuing orders concerned with their departure.

"And your family?"

"Waiting out of doors with Filomene."

"The horses?"

"Saddled and waiting, mademoiselle."

"The scarf and hat?"

"They are there, on that chair, mademoiselle."

M. de Corbal halted beside her at this point in that catechism. She was, he observed, rather pale and a little breathless, but so brisk and determined in manner that wonder grew even as he watched and listened. He was perceiving in her a further display of that spirit which Chauvinière had so much admired.

In riding-boots ridiculously large, but secretly stuffed with hay to make them fit her, she stepped aside to take up the tricolour sash and the plumed and cockaded hat, purloined from Chauvinière who would no longer need them. She returned to proffer them to the Vicomte.

"These are for you."

He recoiled, almost in horror.

"You must wear them, my friend," she insisted. "It is a necessity. Henceforth, you are the Citizen-Representative Chauvinière."

"It will need more than this …" he was beginning.

"I have more." She tapped her breast. "Trust me a little, my friend. Above all do not let us now delay. Come."

He yielded to her peremptoriness and suffered her to assist him to assume the sash of office, and afterwards, to lead him out, Fougereot following with M. de Corbal's valise.

Outside by the horses, visible in the light that streamed through the open door, stood Fougereot's wife and their two big lads and

Filomene. Came brief, but touching farewells between the seigneur and his shrunken family. The Fougereots, all four, were in tears, not only at parting with their Vicomte, but at what else remained to be done. This and the stifled sobbing of Filomene moved him so profoundly that he could not trust himself to speak. In silence he wrung the hand of each in turn, then got to horse. It was Mademoiselle de Montsorbier who spoke for him now.

"You will care for the land," she told them, "and count it your own until monsieur the Vicomte comes to claim it again."

"God send that may be soon!" said Fougereot, and in a choking voice added something which the Vicomte did not understand. "We'll rebuild the house for you."

"God keep you, M. le Vicomte!" cried Fougereot's wife, and the others repeated it after her.

With that valediction ringing in his ears Corbal, still half-bemused, put spurs to his horse, and presently by a path that skirted the little town of Poussignot he was trotting through the dusk with his fair, frail but very resolute companion, their faces set towards Burgundy.

They breasted a slope to the east of the town, and an hour and a half later paused on the summit to breathe their horses, and to look back.

The valley below lay all in darkness. But five miles to westward a flaming beacon split the gloom and drew the eye. It drew more than the eye of M. de Corbal. A moment he gazed, his head craned forward, his breath suspended.

"God of Heaven!" he cried out at last. "That is Corbal. It is on fire." Had he himself been burning at the stake, his voice could hardly have carried more distress.

Mademoiselle at his elbow, sighed before replying.

"Yes, my dear. It is Corbal. Corbal and all that it contains as a funeral pyre to Chauvinière."

Something in her quiet tone recalled Fougereot's cryptic phrase: "We will rebuild the house." He swung in the saddle to peer at her through the gloom.

"You knew!" he cried, almost in reproach.

"I ordered it."

"You ordered it?" Amazement raised his voice. "And they obeyed you?"

"Only because they perceived the need to do so, for your own safety and for theirs."

"The need? What need? And why was I not told?" He was between anger and complaint.

"You might have demurred, and time might have been lost in persuading you. Perhaps, out of a natural love for the house of your fathers, you might have refused to be persuaded until it was too late. Fougereot perceived that, too. Therefore, he obeyed me."

"But the need for this?" he repeated.

"The need to destroy all evidence of what took place, not only to ensure against pursuit, but also to make things safe for your people who remain, and who might otherwise be incriminated. Listen, my dear. By now the Fougereots will be in Poussignot with the tale in which I instructed them. They will relate that returning from the fields at dusk they found the Chateau on fire. That is all they know. Poussignot will surmise a dozen things, amongst them that you have perished in the flames, which they may even suppose – the Fougereots may hint at – that you set alight. They will surmise things, too, on the score of Chauvinière, particularly if it be known to any of them that he went to Corbal this evening. But don't let that trouble you. By dawn we shall be far away."

"You make it clear," he said. "Forgive my dullness." He looked across the valley at the leaping flames, and as he looked his sight grew blurred. "Yes, it was necessary, all things considered. But, oh, my God!"

It was a moment before she answered him, and when she did so she set a hand upon his arm.

"In this world, Raoul, all things worth having must be bought and paid for. That bonfire is the price you pay for life. Is it worthwhile?"

Instantly he swung to her, and cast his weakness from him.

"A thousand times if I am not to be cheated yet. If I am to buy life and love."

"You shall not be cheated, my dear. I have promised you both, and I'll not cheat you of either." She withdrew her hand from his arm, and spoke in another brisker tone. "Let us push on. Henceforth you are the Representative Chauvinière on a mission to Switzerland, and I am your secretary, Antoine."

He sighed, still dubious. "Yes. But if we are called upon to prove it?"

She proffered him a package, wrapped in oiled silk and tied by a ribbon. "You had better carry these," she said. "They are the passports of the Committee of Safety to the Representative Chauvinière and his secretary, commanding all to aid and warning all against hindering them, in the name of the Republic, One and Indivisible. And there are some other papers, also of importance, enjoining obedience upon all civil functionaries. It was prudent of me to have taken the representative's portfolio when I fled from him at La Charité. But I never thought to pass myself off again as his secretary as I never thought to find a substitute for Chauvinière himself, nor while he lived would this have been easy."

He was silent a long time in sheer wonder of her wit and resource. Then he fetched a sigh that ended in a little laugh.

"I should have known better than to suppose that you merely hoped to strike blindly across the frontier. This makes things easy … assured! Oh, it is incredible, as incredible as you are, Cléonie!"

He heard her answering laugh in the dark.

"Let us be moving, dear. We are on surer ground, I think, than your republican nuptials would have provided."

He wheeled his horse to follow her.

"The nuptials surely are also in the arrangement," said he.

Again her laughter answered him, but this time very soft and tender. And the nuptials followed, in Lausanne, a week later, when they found themselves among friends.

Rafael Sabatini

Captain Blood

Captain Blood is the much-loved story of a physician and gentleman turned pirate. Peter Blood, wrongfully accused and sentenced to death, narrowly escapes his fate and finds himself in the company of buccaneers. Embarking on his new life with remarkable skill and bravery, Blood becomes the 'Robin Hood' of the Spanish seas. This is swashbuckling adventure at its best.

The Gates of Doom

'Depend above all on Pauncefort', announced King James; 'his loyalty is dependable as steel. He is with us body and soul and to the last penny of his fortune.' So when Pauncefort does indeed face bankruptcy after the collapse of the South Sea Company, the king's supreme confidence now seems rather foolish. And as Pauncefort's thoughts turn to gambling, moneylenders and even marriage to recover his debts, will he be able to remain true to the end? And what part will his friend and confidante, Captain Gaynor, play in his destiny?

'A clever story, well and amusingly told' – The Times

Rafael Sabatini

The Lost King

The Lost King tells the story of Louis XVII – the French royal who officially died at the age of ten but, as legend has it, escaped to foreign lands where he lived to an old age. Sabatini breathes life into these age-old myths, creating a story of passion, revenge and betrayal. He tells of how the young child escaped to Switzerland from where he plotted his triumphant return to claim the throne of France.

'...the hypnotic spell of a novel which for sheer suspense, deserves to be ranked with Sabatini's best' – New York Times

Scaramouche

When a young cleric is wrongfully killed, his friend, André-Louis, vows to avenge his death. André's mission takes him to the very heart of the French Revolution where he finds the only way to survive is to assume a new identity. And so is born Scaramouche – a brave and remarkable hero of the finest order and a classic and much-loved tale in the greatest swashbuckling tradition.

'Mr Sabatini's novel of the French Revolution has all the colour and lively incident which we expect in his work' – Observer

RAFAEL SABATINI

THE SEA HAWK

Sir Oliver, a typical English gentleman, is accused of murder, kidnapped off the Cornish coast, and dragged into life as a Barbary corsair. However Sir Oliver rises to the challenge and proves a worthy hero for this much-admired novel. Religious conflict, melodrama, romance and intrigue combine to create a masterly and highly successful story, perhaps best-known for its many film adaptations.

THE SHAME OF MOTLEY

The Court of Pesaro has a certain fool – one Lazzaro Biancomonte of Biancomonte. The Shame of Motley is Lazzaro's story, presented with all the vivid colour and dramatic characterisation that has become Sabatini's hallmark.

'Mr Sabatini could not be conventional or commonplace if he tried' – Standard

21770814R00056

Printed in Great Britain
by Amazon